The door between our bedrooms is open. I can see his bed in the distance, the quilt thrown off as though he'd left it in a hurry.

Had I screamed? Had I...?

My eyes return to his, the dregs of my dream still pulsing through my veins...

"Sorry," he says again. He's perched on the edge of my bed. "You sounded distressed."

He looks so concerned, his brow all furrowed, and those eyes... *God*, those eyes... I could lose myself in them a million times over.

"Let me get you some water..."

He's rising up, but I don't want water. I need him out of here because this room, his concern, the *bed*, it's all too intimate. And I don't trust myself not to act on what's been a lifelong dream, a fantasy, one that could so easily become real in the sleepy confines of this room...

"It's okay, Edward," I say. "I don't—"

But he's not listening. He's already heading to the bathroom, and that's when I realize he's wearing nothing but his underwear. The sight steals my voice, my breath...

Dear Reader,

I have the hugest admiration for foster parents—the selfless commitment, the never-ending supply of patience, stability and love for children who need it.

I love a matchmaking tale, especially one that's orchestrated by a loving (read interfering!) grandparent.

And I adore Scotland. Its heritage, beauty, wildlife, castles, lochs... The list goes on.

Bring all these elements together and *My Year with the Billionaire* was born. It's a tale of second chances, the bonds of family, the breaking down of social barriers and realizing that falling in love may be the riskiest but also the biggest, most satisfying adventure of all.

I hope you love Summer and Edward's tale as I did and that it fills you with all the warm fuzzies, too.

Happy reading!

Rachael xx

My Year with the Billionaire

Rachael Stewart

Recycling programs
for this product may
not exist in your area.

ISBN-13: 978-1-335-73682-6

My Year with the Billionaire

Copyright © 2022 by Rachael Stewart

For questions and comments about the quality of this book,
please contact us at CustomerService@Harlequin.com.

Harlequin Enterprises ULC
22 Adelaide St. West, 41st Floor
Toronto, Ontario M5H 4E3, Canada
www.Harlequin.com

Printed in U.S.A.

Rachael Stewart adores conjuring up stories, from heartwarmingly romantic to wildly erotic. She's been writing since she could put pen to paper—as the stacks of scrawled-on pages in her loft will attest to. A Welsh lass at heart, she now lives in Yorkshire with her very own hero and three awesome kids—and if she's not tapping out a story, she's wrapped up in one or enjoying the great outdoors. Reach her on Facebook, Twitter (@rach_b52) or at rachaelstewartauthor.com.

Books by Rachael Stewart

Harlequin Romance

Claiming the Ferrington Empire

Harlequin DARE

Visit the Author Profile page at Harlequin.com.

For Pippa, my sanity xxx

Praise for
Rachael Stewart

PROLOGUE

Edward

I KNOW I SHOULDN'T STARE. That I should keep on walking and pretend I haven't seen. But I can't tear my eyes away.

I also can't believe what I'm seeing.

Summer Evans, my gran's new foster child, is taking a *swim*. I get that it's hot, the summer heatwave unusually oppressive, but a swim…in the *loch*? I've been visiting the castle every year of my life—twenty years and counting—and not once have I considered dipping my toes, let alone diving in headfirst.

I shouldn't be surprised. I've met enough of Gran's foster children to expect the unexpected. But this…

She can't be that much younger than me, yet her actions set her a world apart and I'm entranced. My fear that I might have to dive in and rescue her abating as she gracefully cuts through the water, her easy stroke belying the weight of her clothing. Not that there's much of that either. Just a simple white T-shirt and denim shorts, her trainers abandoned at the end of the rickety wooden dock.

I head to the water's edge, watch the sun play

over the ripples she creates and have the wildest urge to join her.

But wildness isn't in me…

And then she turns and bright blue eyes collide with mine, their flecks of gold glinting up at me as they widen, her gasp drowned out by the water splashing around her.

Now she might need rescuing…

My heart jerks in my chest, failing to settle as her expression lifts, her movements calm and she cracks the widest of grins.

'You must be Edward?'

Her voice rings out across the loch, her accent hard to identify. It's not quite Scottish, not quite English. A mashing together of sorts.

'That's me.' I clear my throat, which feels strangely tight. 'Gran sent me to tell you dinner will be ready in half an hour.'

She cocks her head to the side as she treads water. 'Half an hour. Got it.'

I shift from one foot to the other, feel the weight of her stare, and can't seem to find the inclination to leave. I've done my duty—now I should go. Instead, I find myself asking. 'Do you have a towel I can fetch…?' Because she can't seriously mean to walk back into the house, clothes all wet. 'Or fresh clothes?'

She laughs. 'Does it look like I came prepared?'

She's got you there…

'Not particularly.' Her spontaneity is as enthralling as it is alien to me. 'But I'm not sure you want to be traipsing back through the castle leaving puddles in your wake.'

She closes the distance between us and I take a step back.

'Don't worry…the sun will dry me off soon enough.'

She reaches for the rungs of the makeshift ladder at the dock's edge and I realise she's about to get out…with her top so see-through she might as well be naked.

I spin on my heel, tug my sweater from around my shoulders, eager to give her something, anything, to stop me seeing more than I should. 'You're welcome to use this.'

I offer it up without turning, my brain working overtime as it persists in painting a picture I don't want to see—of her clothes clinging to her every curve, her smile bright, her eyes full of spark…

I blame my intense reaction on my life of late. All work and no play…it's a saying for a reason. I've had my head down for so long I've forgotten that life exists outside of my university dorm. Coming here is meant to be a break from it all, a chance to let off steam—something this Summer looks to be quite proficient at.

I'm accosted by a fierce pang of envy, cut short by her sudden laughter that urges me to turn— though I won't, not until she's covered up.

'You're quite the gentleman.' The jumper slips from my hand into hers.

'I try.' I swallow, my ears attuned to the water dripping over the wooden boards, and I imagine her shaking out her short blonde hair, wringing out her sodden shirt. The slightest droplet catches on my arm and goosebumps prickle beneath the path it takes down my arm.

'You going to stand there for ever?'

'Huh?' Now I turn and look and… What the…? I give a disbelieving cough. 'I didn't mean for you to sit on it.'

'Oh…' She looks down at where my sweater is stretched out beneath her, her palms pressed into the delicate cashmere, her wet denim-clad behind too. 'Sorry.' She winces up at me. 'Would you like it back?'

'Would I…?' I'm unable to finish. My head is shaking as my lips twist up into a smile—the first genuine smile I've felt in ages. 'No. No, I don't want it back.'

'Good.' She grins once more, her eyes going back to the view. The sun lights her up from top to toe, beads of water leaving glistening trails over her bare skin that my eyes are keen to follow. My throat tightens further, my chest too. Is she doing it on purpose?

I tug my gaze back to her face, to where her lashes create dark crescents over her high cheek-bones, and she breathes in deep. She acts like she hasn't a care in the world, but that can't be true. As my mother always says, Gran's foster children come with enough baggage to sink a ship. You steer clear—*well* clear.

'Want to join me?'

She doesn't open her eyes as she says it and I look away, to the far less provocative horizon, and tell myself to walk away, to reset the unfamiliar buzz she's sparked in my veins.

But I don't want to. There's an ease about her, an ease that's also wild and unfettered, and I want to stay in its orbit just a little longer.

I contemplate going back inside, being robbed of her presence, which is as warm as the sun itself, and my blood runs cold. She's Summer through and through, and I lower myself to the dock before my common sense dictates otherwise.

'Was it so hard to decide?' she murmurs, ripe with teasing.

Teasing that has the smile returning to my lips as I rack my floundering brain for a slick retort. I'm not usually this inept with the opposite sex, but then… I've never met a girl quite like her.

She turns away to rummage inside her shoe, draws out a cigarette. 'Want one?'

I screw my face up, the magic somewhat dampened. 'No. Thank you.'

'It's only been in my trainer for a minute or two.'

'It's not the trainer I object to.'

'Ah...' She cocks a brow. 'So it's the smoking. Not the done thing in your hoity-toity circles, hey?'

I know she's mocking me; I can see it in her eyes as she catches the cigarette between her teeth and pulls out a lighter. 'Suit yourself.'

She sparks it up as I watch on—fascinated, disgusted, amazed...

'You know Gran doesn't approve, right?'

Is that really my voice? So gravel-like and hoarse? And why can't I tear my eyes from her lips? The plump bed on which the cigarette rests and the perfect cupid's bow above...all luscious and pink.

She takes a slow puff, wets her lips to torment me further. 'Not my problem.'

A defiant fire comes alive behind her eyes, warring with her relaxed ease and I frown, uncaring that I can see the black outline of her bra through the clinging white T-shirt—who wears black under white anyway?

Someone who doesn't like to conform...a rebel... And heaven knows Gran has seen her fair share of them over the years. Seems Summer is no exception.

'You're living under her care, under her roof, don't you think that makes it your problem?'

She meets my gaze, all steel and ice, and then her eyes trail over me as though she's seeing me properly for the first time and her lips quirk, her eyes warm. 'Are you going to discipline me?'

I bite back a curse, smother the excited kick to my gut—*Definitely* a rebel and *definitely* trouble with a capital T.

Is she toying with me? Mocking me some more? The public schoolboy, born and bred. Not a hair out of place, my chinos and pale blue polo shirt perfectly pressed... Or is she genuinely flirting, liking what she sees?

Whatever the case, there's no answer I can give. None that feels safe and correct. And I'm all about that.

My silence has her laughing softly, releasing me from her provocative stare as she looks to the water and flicks it with her toes. 'How long are you stopping for?'

It takes me a second to trust my voice, another to form a response. 'Didn't Gran say?'

'Nope.'

She settles back on her elbows, stretching her body out languorously, and I'm caught up in her, my brain and voice silenced by the heat that rushes into my veins. I forget myself, forget what we're talking about, and too late, she's caught me looking where I shouldn't. Heat streaks my cheeks, my pulse pounds...

Not that she cares. She's revelling in it. Her breathless chuckle is all flirtatious, the nip she gives the corner of her mouth even more so.

Speak, you fool, before she labels you as one.

'September. I'm staying until September. When term starts up again.'

'Edinburgh Uni, right?'

I nod and she gives a low whistle, her gaze raking back over me. Her own pulse flickers in her throat as her eyes darken. I know that look. I know it and I want to act on it. The urge burns through me even as I acknowledge that it's a line I should not cross…even if it's a line she has probably crossed herself many times over.

'So…' she breaks the heated silence, rakes her teeth over her lower lip '…we have the entire summer together. How fun.'

Swallow. Speak. 'You think so?'

'Don't you?'

Her eyes collide with mine and images dance through my mind. Wrong. Tempting. Crazy. It's like she's projecting her idea of fun at me—but her kind of fun and my kind of fun are not one and the same.

Maybe they should be, the devil on my shoulder argues.

She gives a soft *hmm*. 'You know, my stay here just got a whole lot better.'

I focus on her words and not the heat she's stirring up. 'You sound like it's just a fleeting visit for you?'

She shrugs, but there's an edge to it, an awkwardness that doesn't fit with her confidence. 'It always is.'

I don't contradict her. I don't tell her that Gran's track record of long-term fostering says otherwise. I'll let her believe what she wants to believe until life proves otherwise.

She turns to me then, a curious look in her eye. I wait for her to say something, but nothing comes. Instead her blue eyes draw me in, deeper and deeper still, until I can't quite catch my breath and I'm forced to break her spell.

'What?'

She smiles, her eyes alight with it. 'We really are chalk and cheese, you and I.'

I give a tight laugh. 'That's one way to put it.'

'You say that like it's a bad thing.'

'No, not bad…'

Risky. Because she intrigues me, fascinates me. To the point that my body is overriding my good sense and all the warning signs telling me to keep her at a safe distance.

'What, then?'

I smile as I find my voice, my mind made up. 'Well, to use your phrase, it either makes me as dry as chalk or as pungent as cheese, and personally I don't fancy being classified as either.'

Her laugh is as brilliant as the sun and my body thrives on it.

'Oh, Edward, we're going to get along famously.'

'You think?'

She gives me a playful wink, leans in close, her voice a husky whisper. 'Oh, I know.'

She pinches her lip in her teeth, her eyes fall to my mouth, and I swear I could kiss her…

I want to—my entire body thrums with the energy to do just that—but I don't.

I want something more.

I want to get to know her.

I want to dig beneath the confident rebel front with its hairline fractures and get to the girl beneath.

And now I have the entire summer to do so…

CHAPTER ONE

Summer

'COME ON, come on, come on...'

I drum my fingers against my knee, my eyes hooked on the blazing green digits that make up the minicab's dashboard clock. I'm going to be late—so late. The traffic's bumper to bumper and we're going nowhere.

Is it always like this? It's been years since I've visited Edinburgh—years since I've been in the UK, even. Everything is just so frantic.

I'm used to open spaces—mountains, beaches, bars—and to people who act like they have all the time in the world and the freedom to enjoy it.

Not here, though. Through the drizzle, people are dashing from one building to the next. Suited and booted. Grey and grouchy.

My eyes drift back to the ticking clock and I chew my lip.

I never should've helped the woman with the missing luggage, or the child with the vending machine that wouldn't play ball, or paused to donate some loose change to the busker singing his heart out in the rain before airport security took him down.

But I did…and there's no going back to rewrite history.

I sigh. It feels like the story of my life—only this time it pains me more than usual.

I should have been here a month ago. Not now, and at the request of a man I don't know, on behalf of the only woman I have ever loved. My foster mother. Katherine.

Not that she loved *me*. Not enough to give me the chance to say goodbye.

My nails bite into my palms, their sting worse for the burn behind my eyes.

No, that's not fair.

I know why she didn't tell me.

But it doesn't make it hurt any less.

Katherine was the closest thing to family I have ever known and now she's gone.

It's back to me…*just me*.

I shrug it off. I don't do sad. It's such a waste of life. We only get one, and we have to live it to the full, right? Cram in as much as possible, see the world, no time to pause…

At least that's the way I see it…even if it's making me late right now.

I lean forward and meet the cabby's eye in the rear-view mirror.

'How much longer?'

He gives a shrug. 'Ten minutes. Twenty. They're tearing up roads all over the city—it's carnage.'

I thrust back into my seat, my knees bobbing.

A horn sounds, another chimes in, and I can't take it any more. Even with my luggage I can walk it faster than this. I look at the satnav, see where I need to be.

Rummaging through my satchel for my purse, I pull out some notes and shove them at him. 'It's enough, right?' I gesture to the meter and he nods, twisting in his seat to eye my luggage sceptically.

'But…'

'It's fine. I've got it.'

I shimmy along the seat and shove open the door. It's a relief just to be out in the fresh air again, and for one brief second I raise my face to the rain and breathe in deep, give the hint of a smile as I feel free again. I've spent too long cooped up on planes and public transport, with the journey from Kuala Lumpur seeming to take for ever when it was twenty-four hours tops.

The desire to check in to a hotel and hit a shower is almost enough to see me doing just that. All it would take was a simple call to Mr McAllister to request that the meeting be put off until tomorrow…

Ah, avoidance, thy name is Summer!

I ignore the inner gibe and slam the door closed as the car behind my taxi gives an impatient honk.

'Yeah, yeah…okay.' What is it with this place?

I wave at them and sling my bag onto my back, strike off in the direction of the solicitor's office. One upside to being heavily laden is that people—

those who are looking up from their various de-
vices, at least—clear a path for you. Definitely
the right decision to get out of the cab. Even if the
weather and the exertion will see me turning up
looking less than best.

Less than best… I laugh. As if I even *have* a
best.

Maybe I should have made more of an effort.

Maybe I should have flown in a day earlier, prepared more—physically and mentally.

But then, I've never been one for putting on a
show, and Katherine respected me for that. Why
change now?

And what if he's there?

I falter on the pavement, catch my shoulder on
a streetlamp and wince.

'There's no reason he should be there,' I grumble under my breath, then right my backpack and
my stride.

Whatever it is Mr McAllister wants to pass on,
it doesn't necessary follow that Edward will be in
attendance too. And if he is going to be present,
wouldn't it have been polite for Katherine's solicitor to mention it in his email?

Polite, yes. Necessary, no.

My pulse skips a beat and I grit my teeth. I've
been going round in circles with this ever since
I received the email and I'm sick of it. If he's
there, he's there. I'll simply have to deal with it.
I'm a thirty-eight-year-old woman who knows

her own mind and her own worth. I'm not an insecure eighteen-year-old running scared. And I'm more than capable of standing my ground and having a civilised conversation, in Edward's presence or not.

You weren't the one who was wronged, though...

I grimace, and the man walking towards me takes a wide berth. Not that I can blame him. I must look half crazed. But debating the past—especially *that* part—always sends me a little loopy. My mind races ahead, wondering if he's married now. A father. Happy. Settled.

I feel the answer in my gut. He has to be. A man like him—kind, wealthy, sexy—is an absolute catch. And if he's happy and settled, maybe he'll be grateful that I left the way I did.

Yup, you keep telling yourself that, sugar!

I up my pace and ignore the pressing feeling in my chest that the past is finally catching up with me...

Edward

Charles clears his throat for the umpteenth time and my eyes narrow on the beads of sweat breaking out over his brow. He hurries to dab it dry with his monogrammed handkerchief, but I've seen enough and it's teasing out an uneasy sweat of my own.

Charles is the epitome of cool—level-headed,

dependable, pragmatic. It's why my grandmother chose him to manage the legal affairs of her estate. He wasn't just her lawyer, he was her closest friend too, which makes his discomfort now all the more concerning.

He tries to smile at me, the wrinkles around his grey eyes deepening behind his wire-framed spectacles. He looks like he's stepped out of the nineteen-thirties, his office too, but I'm not here to appraise his dress or choice of décor. I'm here for the reading of my grandmother's will. If only he'd get on with it…

I understand that it's hard for him. Hell, it's hard for us both. But the quicker we get this done with, the better.

It's bad enough that my parents didn't deem the reading important enough to cut their travels short. Enough that for all my grandmother loved and cared for others it's just me sat here now. Me and whoever it is Charles has insisted we wait for. Not that he will tell me. I've asked. He's denied.

Curiouser and curiouser, as my *Alice-in-Wonderland*-loving grandmother would have said.

I don't return his edgy smile. I adjust my tie and glance at the old grandfather clock that has been a feature of this room for as long as I have known him.

Twenty minutes late. Just how long does he

want to wait? I have places to be, people to see, distractions to pursue…

'We're both busy, Charles.'

I drag my gaze back to his, ignore the weight of the lie. Because the truth is I'm not busy enough. It's been a month since Gran died—a month. And nothing can fill the void she's left behind. And I've tried. I've tried everything.

Though none of my grief slips into my voice. It never pays to appear weak. My mother taught me that and life reinforced it. 'I don't see why we can't get this over and done with now.'

He chokes on thin air and wets his lips—the gesture tests my patience and my nerves further.

'I'm sure they will be here very soon. They promised they would be. And I promised your grandmother I would abide by their wishes.'

'If I'm to be made to wait for this person, surely I deserve a name?'

My ears are primed for their identity…yet, nothing. What's he so afraid of?

'Come now, Charles. I must know them. Unless you've managed to dig up some distant relative that no one has ever heard of and declare Katherine's entire—'

'I'm so sorry I'm late!'

The breathless voice permeates the heavy oak door to Charles's office and the man himself shoots up out of his seat, wiping his palms down his trousers as the door opens on his secretary.

'Miss Evans has arrived, Mr McAllister.'

'Thank you, Tracy.'

He's already striding forward, his smile warm as he looks past Tracy to the woman I've heard but haven't yet set eyes on.

Miss Evans?

Who on earth is…?

The faintest of bells ring in the deepest, darkest recesses of my mind… The slight rasp to that feminine tone…the unidentifiable accent…

I rise and turn, good manners overriding my mental flurry as I seek to greet our new arrival, but the ground shifts beneath my feet, my vision narrowing until all I see is her.

Summer.

It's not… It can't be…

I force my body to straighten, smooth out my tie on impulse as my head refuses to believe what my eyes are seeing. At first all I register is an abundance of blonde hair and bronze skin— far too much skin for autumn in Scotland—and clothing that seems so mismatched it's like she's walked into a charity shop and paid no heed to size nor colour. Her walking boots are as worn as her backpack, which is almost as big as her and likely weighs much more.

Where the hell does she think she is? Her whole get-up is better suited to a trek across the sunny beaches of Bali than the streets of Edinburgh in the damp and dreary depths of autumn.

Does she not realise what season we're in? Does she not care that she looks so out of place?

Did she ever?

My head taunts me, reminds me, teases me.

This is Summer, who never cared for anyone's opinion but her own.

And that's when I meet her gaze and it truly hits home. Summer. Summer Evans. She's the person we've been waiting for. She's the person Gran insisted be here for this.

A thousand memories surge forth as my heart stutters in my chest.

The grin she gives me is accentuated by lines that suggest she smiles often. The nose that has seen a bump or two lifts marginally and her eyes… her eyes transport me back twenty years, to those same bright blue eyes, the same rebellious grin…

I snap my gaze away.

'What the hell is she doing here?' I fire at Charles, and his sweat makes a prompt return, his smile falters.

'Well, if you'll both sit down,' he blusters, 'I can explain just that.'

'It's a pleasure to see you too,' she directs at me, and although her voice is strong, her eyes show a hint of what I'd like to think is remorse.

Though she hasn't got the heart for remorse.

I'm the one choking on thin air now, and she has the decency to look away, to hesitate. She combs unsteady fingers through her hair, sweeps the rain-dampened strands off her flushed cheeks and she secures it back with some brightly coloured cloth.

Where on earth has she come from? Where has she been all this time? And, more importantly, why is she here?

She grips her backpack tightly now, her knuckles flashing white, and I realise the room has fallen silent and all eyes are on me. Waiting on me.

Her throat bobs, her lashes flutter. 'Well, shall we sit?'

Sit? With *her*? To hear my grandmother's will? This has to be a joke. Some weird, twisted joke.

'Yes, let's sit.'

Charles is all over the idea, ushering her to a seat, helping her deposit her bag on the floor, and I'm… I'm stood there like some bloody lemon. My eyes tracking her, devouring her. Does the woman not own a coat? It's raining cats and dogs out there and her bare arms shine with it, her clothes cling to her skin…

And just like that I'm back at the loch over two decades ago, and the fire is as immediate as it is unwelcome.

'Can I get you a drink, Miss Evans?'

Charles persists in trying to make her welcome… trying to make up for my obvious hostility, I'm sure.

'A coffee? Tea? Water…?'

I can almost sense Gran looking down on me in disapproval, her *tut-tut-tut* echoing through my soul.

If Gran wants her here, my mind tries to reason, *you need to play nice.*

'Water would be lovely,' she murmurs softly, and I want to shut myself off from the way her voice sings through my blood. 'Thank you.'

'Sparkling? Still?'

'Either's fine,' she says, her eyes returning to me, hesitant, wary...

She's completely out of her depth.

It should make me feel better.

It doesn't.

It does make me move, though.

Dragging a hand over my face, I return to my seat and force normal service to resume—the projection of an outward calm strong enough to mask the inner storm.

Oh, Gran, what have you done?

CHAPTER TWO

Summer

'GRAN'S DONE *WHAT*?'

I leap a little in my seat at Edward's outburst. I'm not sure what's worse: his initial greeting or his response to the will.

Not that I can blame him for either.

And I'm just as stunned. Speechless, in fact. Not a trait I'm experienced in, let alone know how to handle. But I'm still struggling to believe we're in the same room together…never mind the unbelievable news Mr McAllister has just delivered.

'Would y-you like me to re-read it from the beginning?'

McAllister dabs at his forehead, his wrinkles deepening. Poor man. Edward is fierce. Like, seriously fierce. The sharp cut of his deep blue suit adds to his severity, and his carefully groomed brown hair is unmoving in its swept-back style, the hard angle to his designer stubble precise and accentuating his prominent cheekbones and strong jaw.

Gone is the twenty-year-old I met all those years ago. The clean-shaven, ex-public schoolboy with his foppish hair, quiet, reserved smiles and sweet nature.

This is a man with the full weight of his years, wealth and success behind him. Not to mention his obvious dislike of me…

'No. No, I don't need you to read it from the beginning, Charles. I understood. I just—'

His chocolate-brown eyes flit to me, razor-sharp, and my heart gives an involuntary flip. I don't even have time to recover before he's looking back at McAllister, accusation flaring in his depths.

'She can't have been thinking straight. You were supposed to…' he waves a hand at the man '…make sure she was in her right mind when she made such decisions.'

'Edward!' I erupt, driven by my innate need to defend her. 'Don't you dare question Katherine's mind; she was perfectly sane.'

'Really?'

His eyes return to me and I can't breathe for the emotion I see there. Anger. Hatred. Pain…

He clenches the end of the armrest closest to me, the veins in his hand popping, his entire body emanating a physical strength he didn't possess before.

'And what would you know of her mind when you haven't seen her in twenty years?'

Bullseye—he might as well have thrown a dart straight through my grieving heart.

'I've always been around,' I say quietly, my cheeks burning with the direct hit.

'Around?' His mouth lifts into a chilling one-sided smile. 'Is that what you call it?'

'Now, now...'

McAllister comes to my rescue. I half expect him to add *children* to the end and inwardly cringe. I don't need him to fight my battles. Especially in front of Edward—*against* Edward.

'Can we focus on the necessary? Katherine knew this would come as a...how shall I put it?...a shock. But she was very clear in her request, and felt it was in *both* your interests to see the conditions of her will through to fruition.'

His voice softens and yet strengthens as he speaks, as if he's warming up to the idea as he watches us closely. I don't know what he sees in us to warrant such sudden positivity. Maybe there's more than just water in the crystal glass he's drinking from.

I take a sip from my own glass, wishing it really was something stronger.

'You were friends once,' he adds into the strained silence. 'I think Katherine thought you could readily be so again.'

'And what if we can't?' I say, ignoring the pang his words evoke. 'Stick to the terms, I mean?'

Beside me Edward makes a sound behind his fist—was that a snort? I give him the side-eye, but his gaze is fixed on McAllister.

'Yes. What she said...'

The man clears his throat, studies the papers before him—more to avoid our eyes, I'm sure.

'If one of you leaves before the year is up, the estate goes to the other party.'

'And if we both leave?' Edward presses.

'Well, then it becomes a bit more complicated. Katherine has outlined a careful segregation of the estate, detailing specific areas that are to be donated to local businesses and charities. The—'

'Glenrobin will be *segregated*?' Edward chokes out the last word with the same shock I feel. Was I wrong about Katherine? Had she been mentally unsound? Had I missed it? Paid too little attention?

The guilt rises as Edward continues, 'But that castle, that entire estate, has been in my family for generations.'

'And of course Katherine would like it to remain that way.'

McAllister actually smiles now as he stacks the papers neatly—is the man delirious?

'So, as you can see, it is in your interests to adhere to the terms set out in the will.'

'And what happens after a year?' I ask. 'What then?'

'After you have lived there for one year you can do whatever you wish with your share. Sell it to the other party, donate it, keep it—so long as you both agree.'

'This is ridiculous.'

'That's the first sensible thing that's been said all morning…' Edward mutters, and I flick him a look—*not helping!*—before going back to McAllister and the problem at hand.

'So, just to be clear, Edward's mother inherits a cash sum and the house in London. The rest—the estate, the staff, the heirlooms of Glenrobin—she's bequeathed to us?'

'Along with a sum of money to supplement the income the estate generates to aid with its running costs. The sum should be enough to last for many years to come.'

I nod, numbly. 'A fifty-fifty split between Edward and me?'

'Precisely.'

Edward clears his throat, his eyes pinning the other man down. 'And what if *she* decides to sell it to the highest bidder when the year is over?'

My stomach rolls at the very idea. Rolls even more at his obvious belief that I would do such a thing.

Does he not realise I'm on his side? I *know* I don't deserve this inheritance. I don't even deserve to be sat in the same room as him, hearing Katherine's last wishes. For all my love for her, I wasn't her blood. I wasn't her true family. No matter how much she tried to make me so.

'I asked you a question, Charles.'

But McAllister is watching me. Worrying about me. I can see it in his sympathetic grey eyes. Something else I don't deserve—the man's sympathy.

Unease creeps down my spine…goosebumps break out across my skin.

'Charles!'

The man comes alive, his eyes flicking to Edward, admonishing him. 'In that case you can refuse, as would be your right. Any sale of the assets must be agreed between the two of you.'

Edward nods. 'And the money that comes with the estate? How exactly does that work?'

McAllister stares at Edward long and hard. 'I'm sure you will find a way to make it work, Mr Fitzroy. Katherine asked me to be involved as much or as little as you need. That includes tracking expenditure if it will help you to focus on setting up home amicably. But Katherine did hope that, given time, you would be quite capable of managing it all between yourselves.'

'"Setting up home"?' Edward's upper lip curls, and his voice is devoid of any depth as the phrase revolves around my mind, races through my heart.

I don't have a home. Never have, never will. Glenrobin Castle was the closest I ever got. Eighteen months I stayed. Grew attached. To the grounds, to the people, to Katherine…to Edward.

And then it started to suffocate me. The panic. The *When will it end?*

All good things have an expiry date. I learned that at a very young age. And it's far better for them to end on my terms than to be at someone else's mercy.

But I hadn't been able to let Katherine go.

And she knew it.

Was that what this was? Was she trying to give me roots? Gifting me a home in death that I couldn't possibly say no to…? It was sick, twisted, manipulative…and it had Katherine's benevolent heart all over it.

'I know this is a lot to take in.' McAllister is filling the strained silence. 'Perhaps if you'd each take the paperwork away, read over it and come back to me with any questions you may have? I will make myself available to you any time you need. Katherine was my dearest friend, my longest client too. This isn't just my job…it's personal.'

Edward gives him a grim smile before turning to look at me, a thousand questions burning behind those rich brown eyes that have haunted my dreams for so long.

I wonder what it would take to have them look at me like they did before. With laughter, with warmth, with—

Leave it alone, Summer! You left for a reason. You ran for a reason. Those reasons haven't gone away.

'Here.' McAllister slides an envelope to each of us. 'She left you each a letter.'

I manage a sad smile, my fingers trembling as I reach for it. The family crest to the bottom right of the ivory embossed paper triggers an ache deep within that I find impossible to ignore. 'Thank you.'

'Is there anything more you'd like to ask?'

I shake my head.

He looks at Edward, whose eyes are trained on the envelope clutched in my hand.

'Mr Fitzroy?'

'No. Nothing that will make sense of this at any rate.'

McAllister gives a grim smile. 'I understand. But rest assured, your grandmother thought long and hard about this. She was never one to make such decisions lightly, as well you know.'

Edward's eyes flash, but his words are measured, 'No. She wasn't.'

'As for your mother—do let me know if I can help relay all this to her. I'm surprised she declined my invitation to be present today.'

'I'm not.'

Edward's tone is clipped as he reaches forward and takes up his letter, tucking it inside his jacket. He's all action now, as though he's made a decision only he is privy to.

'Thank you, Charles, we'll see ourselves out.'

'I'd offer to escort you to the estate…'

McAllister is looking at me, but it's Edward who speaks. 'That won't be necessary.'

Edward's already on his feet and I follow suit, frustrated that he's talking for both of us but too numb to argue. I shove the envelope into my satchel and sling the bag over my chest, hurry to tug my backpack from Edward's reaching grasp.

'I've got it,' I say, throwing it onto my back, my eyes colliding with his in challenge.

He clenches his jaw, gives me a brisk nod and gestures for me to lead the way.

I take my time, refusing to dance to his tune.

It's not like I planned any of this.

It's not like it's my fault.

'Thank you, Charles.' His tone warms with respect for the older man and a modicum of gratitude. 'I'll be in touch.'

McAllister stands, his smile heightened by relief that the meeting is done with, I'm sure. He offers his hand to me and I take it.

'It's good to see you again, Summer.'

'Thank you.'

I shake his hand, return his smile, but inside I'm questioning the 'again'. Have we met before? I guess it stands to reason I might have met him at one of Katherine's many social functions at the estate—many non-social too. But I only had eyes for one man back then.

I suck in a breath as I turn to face that man now. He's still waiting, his brooding presence as heavy as the rainclouds outside. He dominates the room, dominates me, and I stifle a shudder. Why does he have the power to make me feel so small and weak?

Wrong. He makes you feel vulnerable, and that's something else entirely.

I'm known for my strength, my decisiveness, my ability to face a challenge head-on. It's time I started acting like me again. But before I do, I need space without him in it. Space to consider Katherine's wishes and figure out a game plan. A plan that will keep my brain engaged and my heart locked away.

Question is, will he give it to me?

I straighten my spine and stride past him. I can feel his eyes boring through my backpack into me. My skin is alive with his proximity, my heart too… Getting space physically might not be an issue but mentally, emotionally…?

Edward

She's surprisingly quick down the Georgian staircase, the backpack failing to hinder her in the slightest. It would be impressive if not for the fact that I know she's running from me.

Again.

Once outside, she shows no sign of slowing, no awareness of me behind her…

Where's she heading in such a hurry?

Anywhere you're not…

'Leaving without saying goodbye?'

She freezes on the stone steps and her bag lifts with her shoulders. She blows out a breath before turning to eye me over her shoulder. 'Look, Edward—'

'Don't worry, Summer, you have form for it. I'm hardly going to get offended now.'

She nips her lip, blue eyes flitting between me and the street—her escape.

'But we *do* need to talk.'

'Right now I need space to think.'

I shove my hands into my pockets, try to ignore the pang of her dismissal and the dogged desire to stay in her orbit. *Dammit.* How can twenty years go by and that frustrating need to be near her in spite of everything remain? An intrinsic need that runs so deep it's as much a part of me as the blood pumping through my veins.

'When, then?'

'Soon.'

'How soon?'

'I don't know, Edward!' she blurts, vibrant and alive in her exasperation. 'This whole thing has come as a huge shock and I need to get my head on straight before I can have a sensible conversation with you about it.'

'Very well,' I say. 'Where are you staying?'

'What does that matter?'

'I'll send the car to pick you up when you're ready to talk.'

'That won't be necessary.'

'Tell that to Gran's driver. He'll already be contemplating his future now the estate is under new management.'

She gives a shake of her head, a bitter laugh. 'I hardly think he wants to drive all the way down from the Highlands to ferry me around.'

'It's not about want—it's his job. It's what the estate pays him for.'

She laughs some more and my already frayed nerves snap. 'I'm glad you find this so amusing.'

She huffs at me, raises her brows to the heavy sky above. 'You're a fool if you think my laughter stems from humour, Edward.'

She shakes her head, takes the last step down and turns to look up at me. I steel myself for whatever she has to say. I steel myself against the warmth that pulses through me at having her so close again. Against the age-old anger and hurt that wants to resurrect itself even though its ancient history.

But now I have Gran's betrayal to add to the mix.

'We'll talk at the estate,' I say. It's an order, not a request. 'It's where we'll be living after all.'

My skin crawls as I acknowledge the truth of it. I feel my heart beating harder, faster, daring her to deny me.

'OK.'

I swallow, ignoring the kick to my pulse that her surprising agreement triggers. 'Good.'

'But I'll get to the estate under my own steam. When are you intending to leave?'

I stare off into the distance. The hustle and bustle of Edinburgh is a relief from her and the pressure building inside my head, my chest. Why is it so hard to breathe with her around? To concentrate and think clearly?

Maybe she's right to demand some space—some time apart before we discuss a way forward. A way that gets her out of my life for good with as little of my grandmother's estate as possible...

'Soon.' My resolve builds with my thoughts. 'I have some business to deal with here first.'

'OK...' She's already stepping away. 'I'll message to let you know when I'm ready to talk.'

'Won't you need my number for that?'

She pauses, her cheeks colouring as she inches back to me, her hand rummaging in her pocket. Her eyes don't quite meet mine as she passes me her phone, and for some unknown reason—probably the masochist in me—I let our fingers touch and feel the age-old connection warm me. Tease me.

I'm as attuned to her sharp intake of breath as I am my own, and I see the fire behind her eyes as they lift to mine, dizzying in their intensity. A thousand long-buried wants grapple to the surface and I want to pull her to me. I want to do what I didn't have the nerve to all those years ago...

And then her hand is snatched away and I'm

jarred back to reality—it's all in me, not her. I'm the one wanting, feeling more than I should…

I clench my jaw, grip her phone tight, key in my number and dial it so that I have her number too, then thrust it back at her.

'Thank you.' She eyes me warily, wets her lips. 'Goodbye, Edward.'

Goodbye, Edward. The simple phrase launches the past into the present with painful clarity. *Now* I get a goodbye…only twenty years too late.

She starts to walk away and anger rears up… ugly, bitter, cold.

'Summer…?'

She pauses, turning just enough to look at me. 'Yes?'

I breathe in her beauty and feed the pain that is very real and very present. 'You may have found a home in Glenrobin once, and Gran may have gifted it to you again, but I'm not her. And I'll find a way around this if it's the last thing I do.'

Her eyes widen and I turn before she can creep beneath my shield anew. I don't care if I've hurt her—I *don't*… Although the nails slicing through my palms tell me otherwise.

I walk away before I surrender to the guilt, and raise my shoulders against the knowledge that Gran will be turning in her grave.

I have myself to protect in the land of living, Gran, surely you can see that?

As for Summer… She doesn't get to leave for

twenty years—no goodbye, no nothing—and then come back with a claim on the estate. My family's estate. She doesn't.

And it's just the claim on the estate you're worried about...?

It's as though Gran is in my head, goading me into acknowledging the true source of my unease, and I thrust a hand through my hair.

In the distance, my driver steps out of the car, races around to the boot and pulls out an umbrella. Too late. I'm soaked through. And I hadn't even noticed. Not the rain beating down, nor the wetness that's seeped through to my skin.

I wave him away, much preferring the drumming beat of the rain to the panicked staccato of my heart.

CHAPTER THREE

Summer

MY FINGERS HOVER over the keyboard. I've typed and deleted his name several times over, with my tap-tap-tapping getting more and more aggressive if the looks from nearby café-goers are any indication.

Or maybe I'm just more sensitive to their presence because I feel like what I'm doing is wrong.

Nosy. *Gossip Girl*-esque. Wrong.

I'd have done it in the privacy of my hotel room, but it turns out their services don't include free Wi-Fi. So now I'm here, propping up a café bar, with my intent stare on my laptop, my search going nowhere.

I haven't looked him up in a decade. I knew enough from Katherine to understand he was doing well; I didn't need to taunt myself with more. Especially not the gazillion visual hits bound to ensue.

The media appeal of the Fitzroys knows no bounds. Good-looking to a fault, his father's English aristocratic roots and his mother's high society breeding make them regular fodder for the press. Edward is no exception.

But the twenty-two-year-old man I left behind

and the man he is now, all suited and booted and so very severe, couldn't appear more different.

And it has nothing to do with age or his impressive frame that suggests he works out—a lot! There's something else. Something dark and dangerous and deeply unsettling.

That'll be his hatred for you.

I throw off the barb. I don't want to believe it. I want to believe it's part and parcel of the man he is now.

He always had an edge, a way of standing out among his peers. Quiet, reserved…his sharp intellect and wit demanding a certain level of respect. But respect and fear aren't one and the same and McAllister had acted like he feared him.

Or was it all about me? His reaction? The lawyer's discomfort? Were they all because of me? Is he all fluffy bunnies and nicey-nice when I'm not around?

No, I don't want to believe it.

But neither do I truly want to believe he's as cold and ruthless as he appeared. Even his accent was clipped, his Scottish lilt indistinct.

And what of the way he touched my hand, held my eye, singed me to my very toes with blatant desire seconds before he delivered his parting remark and cut me to the core.

I shudder and shake it off. I should've known he would be there. I should have prepared myself better, scoured the internet for all the info I could find…

So get it done.

His name glares back at me, the cursor blinking next to it, and I strike 'enter' far harder than necessary. My eyes narrow—part-wince, part-studying—as the results appear.

Billionaire… Billionaire… Billionaire.

The word is on repeat. With every mention of his name it's there, alongside a whole list of accolades, and I'm scrolling and scrolling…

British media magnate…tech and finance entrepreneur…philanthropist…crypto-currency…social entrepreneur…company founder…net worth…

I swallow… He really is worth billions. *Actual* billions. I shouldn't be surprised…not really…but that kind of wealth…?

Just how ruthless did one have to be to achieve such heights?

How hungry for money?

For me, the stuff's a necessary evil. I live each day to the next, never knowing where my next adventure will take me, let alone the source of my next paycheque. Don't get me wrong. I'm not irresponsible. I always put enough aside to ensure I'm a burden to no one—

A burden?

I choke on a laugh. There's no one I could be a burden *to*. The only person I ever let myself care about is gone… Well, not quite the only one. The other is staring back at me on the screen, his static image enough to make my body warm. Doesn't matter that I know he hates me, wants rid of me…

Not that I can blame him.

I left without a goodbye.

I left, and now he's suffering the injustice of having to share his inheritance with me.

And what if he's married? What if he has an entire family to uproot? Would Katherine really do that to him?

I'm already typing *Edward Fitzroy Wife*.

Enter.

So many pictures, so many articles, all pondering his personal life. Connecting him to society's finest: tech legends, business moguls…women on a par with himself. In looks and brains. Each one so much more than I could ever be.

The past rushes forth, the pain surprisingly acute, and I close my eyes, shut out the memory determined to surface.

You're good enough just the way you are. You have nothing to prove. No one to impress.

I breathe through the tightness, force my fists to relax.

Leave the past in the past and focus on the present, on the situation you're in…

I reach for my mocha, take a sugary soothing sip, and dare to scroll further…

Wait!

The hot liquid catches in my throat and I cough it up, my lips quivering over a hit.

No.

I click the headline, unable to resist:

> *A Good-Looking Guy, Successful and*
> *of a Certain Age, Still a Bachelor…*
> *Is our Dashing Fitzroy Gay?*

It's an inevitable article, born of an inevitable question, but it tickles me. That's one question I'm sure I know the answer to. We might not have crossed that line, but the look in his eye back then…the look in his eye only yesterday, so strong it rose above the hatred… No, he's not gay.

I only wish I could be as sure about Katherine's intentions. And I know the letter will help explain, but I haven't been able to open it. It's there now, poking out from beneath my laptop, but each time I reach for it my stomach turns over and my fingers refuse to do my bidding. Guilt and grief holding me hostage.

I should have come back sooner. I should have known she was sick. I should have… I should have…

My eyes sting and I grit my teeth, swallow. I'm

in a public place, it's no time for tears, but I'm confused…*so* confused.

'What were you thinking, Katherine?' I whisper.

'You mean you don't know?'

I jump as the deep, sexy drawl resonates through my core, my eyes widening as I spin on my stool. 'Edward!'

I can't believe my eyes…but my body does. It's already a hive of activity, my pulse spiking, my mouth drying out.

Does he have to be so goddam sexy all the time? The collar of his herringbone coat is pulled high, his dark wintry look crisp and elegant. His chestnut hair is immaculate, despite the chilling breeze outside, and his eyes, that mouth…

He already looks angry about something. The pink in his cheeks from the biting wind is the only sign of humanity in his face that's set like stone.

'What are you—? Why are you—? How did you know I'd be here?'

And why do I have to sound like a tongue-tied schoolgirl with an impossible infatuation?

Because it's how you feel.

His lips twitch, the sensation inside me deepens—is he laughing at me?

No, I doubt the man ever laughs these days…

'I have my ways.'

'I bet you do.' Every one of them involving the cash he appears to have an endless supply of…it doesn't explain *why* he's here though. 'And you're here because…?'

He says nothing and my brows nudge north. Maybe I'm not the only one struggling with their words. Maybe he's just as disorientated by my presence…

And maybe you're losing it more than you think!

'I'm here to see you.'

'Stating the obvious much?'

Fire flickers behind his eyes and my heart leaps into my throat—*do you want to poke the bear?*

'I mean—'

'I want to apologise,' he says over me.

'You—?' I frown, taken aback…surely I didn't hear him right. 'You what?'

'I want to apologise.'

And now he sounds like a robot…and I'm still not sure I understand. 'You want to *apologise*?'

'I do.'

'You…*do*…?'

My chin tucks in as I look up at him and he makes an exasperated sound that has me wanting to laugh.

'Please don't make this any harder than it needs to be.'

'*Harder?* Begging your pardon, Edward, but did you rush off for a lobotomy last night or something?'

His frown is instantaneous, and the way it

makes his lower lip pout…too appealing, too distracting. But an apology…?

I face him full-on, my confidence growing as relief seeps through my limbs. It has to be a good sign, right?

He drags in a breath…pockets his hands. 'It was a shock; *I* was in shock. I had no idea Gran was going to do this.'

'And you think *I* did?'

A V forms between his brows and I have the ridiculous urge to smooth it away, a delicate gesture that is so at odds with his sheer masculinity.

'Well…didn't you?'

'God, no! If I had I would've told her to her face she'd lost the plot.'

A hint of a smile touches his lips and I yearn for a full-blown grin, the slightest of chuckles—anything to suggest the Edward I once knew is still in there somewhere.

'You'd have been given quite the ear-bashing if you'd tried.'

I give a soft huff, feel bittersweet memories choking up my throat, and I swallow. 'She always was deft at saying just the right thing to get me to fall in line.'

His posture softens along with his eyes as the past shifts between us, wrapping around us, uniting us.

'Well, if you would go around flouting the rules…'

'Says the guy who couldn't flout a single one without breaking out in hives.'

And just like that he tenses, every one of his honed muscles drawing tight.

'I've changed since then.'

It's like he's in my head, but the words are leaving my lips before I can stop them. 'So I can see…'

And the real me—the daring, the confident, usually unperturbed one—comes to life and I let my eyes trail over him, full of provocation. I don't care that I'm eating him with my eyes. I want to devour him. I want him to burn like I do. I want my presence to stir into life that part of him those women on the Internet have enjoyed over the intervening years…

'This apology…' I force my eyes back to his, spy the reciprocal fire I've succeeded in provoking. 'I'm still waiting.'

He scoffs and it doesn't become him… It becomes the old him, though, and I suck my lips in to stop the smile that wants to break free.

'Ever the demanding one, Summer.'

'Well, if you will leave a lady waiting…'

I see the retort burning in his gaze—*I see no lady here*—but he doesn't say it. Twenty years ago he would have come straight out with it. Just for fun. Why not now?

Maybe he's more attuned to what sent me running all those years ago than I give him credit for…or maybe he's just grown up.

In either case, the humour and the passion are no more. I'm chilled to the bone.

'This apology?'

His eyes sharpen and I wonder if he's sensed the shift…

He clears his throat, gives an abrupt nod. 'I *am* sorry, Summer. I've had time to reflect. I've also had time to read the letter Gran left…have you read yours?'

He spies it poking out on the table and I shake my head. 'Not yet.'

I see the question in his eyes—*why not?*

'I—I'll get to it when I'm ready.'

'Right…'

There's a pause, and I know he's pondering my reaction, and all the emotions that feed my hesitancy start to clamber for attention.

'So, you've read the letter and…?' I throw the focus back on him, smother the inner turmoil.

'And I don't agree with what she has done, nor much of what she put in her letter, but this is her last request and I will respect it…to a point.'

'To a point…?' I repeat numbly, wondering how far that point will go. Do I get a tent in the garden? A toilet in the outhouse? Are we really doing this? Living together?

My heart starts to race…

'Yes. And the sooner we can talk it through the better.'

I can't respond. There are no words for this…
this craziness.

'So, come with me?'

'Wait. What?' Panic kickstarts my voice. 'Come
with you where?'

'To the estate. We can use the travel time to talk.'

'But I… *When?*'

'This afternoon.'

'But…'

Swallow, Summer. Breathe.

It's too soon. I've not had enough time to think.
To process.

He dips his head, leans that little bit closer, and
his cologne reaches me, floods my senses… Why
does he have to smell so good too?

'But what?'

Close your gaping mouth and answer the man.

'But it's a couple of hundred miles away.'

'And? Surely spending the journey with me is
not that awful a prospect…'

A shiver runs down my spine as I catch the hint
of mockery in his rich, dulcet tones.

'We used to enjoy one another's company once,
Summer. I'm sure we can at least be civil for that
amount of time.'

The blood seeps from my cheeks and I bluster
out a laugh. 'Is that supposed to make the offer
more appealing?'

He gives a wry smile.

'No, I don't suppose it does. But I'm sure it benefits the planet in some way, us combining our journey. And I know how much you care for that.'

'Not when there's a train heading that way and…'

Hang on, my voice trails off as my eyes narrow. My eco-warrior efforts came after Glenrobin… after him…

Has he been reading up on *me*? Or is it something Katherine said? What does he know? What has he seen? What's in the public domain? Protest rallies—sure. The odd arrest—maybe.

Oh, God. A certain picture sears my brain and my cheeks are aflame before I can erase it. Please don't let him have seen *that* one…

'Fine,' I rush out. 'When do you—*we*—leave?'

'I'll pick you up at two.'

I wet my lips, my voice failing me again.

'Is that a problem?' he asks.

No. Yes. No. But it's only a few hours away from now…

'Not at all. Two p.m. it is.'

'Great.'

'Great.'

Awkward…

'Is there anything else?' I say, when he still doesn't move.

'No.' He comes alive. 'I'll see you later.'

He turns to leave and then hesitates. My heart leaps. *What now?*

He looks back at me, a curious glint in his eye. 'I'm not, by the way.'

'You're not what?'

His eyes flit to the screen of my laptop and to my horror I'm still on *that* page, with the headline blazing—*Is our Dashing Fitzroy Gay?*

Of all the articles it had to be that one…

Floor, swallow me now!

'I'll take the dashing, though.'

Something glitters behind those chocolate-brown eyes…something that triggers a thousand flutters inside me, each one contending with the mortifying burn.

'Goodbye, Summer.'

And then he's gone, and I want to stick my head and my nether regions in the nearest freezer. Maybe the café will have one out back big enough to take my entire body if I ask nicely enough…

I opt for slamming the laptop closed and pressing my forehead into its solid metal top.

Edward

I pull open the door to the street and can't resist one last look.

She's face-planted on her laptop and laughter bubbles up inside me, its force as surprising as its presence. I shake my head, step out, grateful for the chill in the morning air.

Nothing about this is funny.

Nothing at all.

She's been back in my life less than twenty-four hours and already turned it on its head. No. Correction. Gran has done that. And as much I loved her, respected her, on this she couldn't have called it more wrong.

Or hurt me any more than she has.

It's not about the money. It's about love and loyalty and my ancestral home. How could she do this? Gift half of it to a woman who's been MIA for twenty years? How could she bring her back into my life and risk exposing me to that kind of pain again?

Betrayed and broken, I have no idea how to fix the way I feel. But I'll stay in control and buy myself the necessary time to eradicate her from my life for good. I have my advisors looking into the terms of the will—if there's a loophole, they will find it.

There's no blood connection and no bond... The woman didn't even make it back for Gran's funeral. What kind of person claims to care and doesn't even turn up to say goodbye?

I clutch the letter in my coat pocket and swallow down the rising sickness, walk away before I storm back inside the café and demand that she tell me.

Now isn't the time or the place. Glenrobin is.

My jaw is throbbing by the time I enter the foyer of my Scottish headquarters, the double-height entrance enhanced by its glass front, white-tiled floor and flashes of chrome. Some might say it's clinical—to me it means business. A space for focus and success. Success I've worked damned hard for, proving that I'm more than just my father's name… My father's title.

And look at Summer now…being gifted a fortune so vast it could feed a small nation and having done nothing to deserve it, too.

Well, over my dead body.

Sorry, Gran.

CHAPTER FOUR

Summer

> *Dearest Summer,*
> *I know this will come as a shock, but you know me: I never do anything without careful consideration. As the saying goes, there's method in my madness, so please bear with me and the terms of my will. I'm not going to play the emotional blackmail card. I'm only going to ask that you give this old woman the benefit of the doubt and humour me, if you will.*
> *And, yes, I'm smiling as I write that.*
> *Now for the serious bit. And please don't groan—it doesn't become you.*
> *I see the way you spend your life, running from one thing to the next, never settling in one place long enough to put down roots. I worry that if you're not careful life will pass you by, and you will never pause long enough to feel what it is to be content, to be happy, to be loved...*
> *It's my greatest regret that neither you nor Edward ever had a true home. One filled with love and laughter as it should be. Oh, I tried—heaven knows I tried. And I suppose you can say that this is my last hurrah...to try and give you both what you've never had.*

Why together?

Because you belong together, and it's high time you realised it.

Call me an old romantic—call me whatever you like—but this is my way of knocking your heads together from above. I should have done it years ago, but I hoped that life would do it for me. Well, life has had its chance and I'm out of mine. So this is it.

Look after yourself, and each other. I believe with all my heart that this is an opportunity for you both to forge a better path to happiness. Please take it.

All my love and hope for the future,

Gran x

I PRESS MY fist to my mouth, fend off the sob that wants to erupt. The sob that's also a laugh, that's also a disbelieving choke.

The carefully crafted words blur with my tears and I lift the sheet away before the first droplet can ruin the ink.

At least I understand her thinking now...

Understand it, yes.

But agree...?

Me and Edward.

It's just not possible.

It wasn't back then. It certainly isn't now.

'I'm sorry, Katherine,' I say into the empty hotel room, wishing I was wrong, wishing she was right, wishing the dream could be real even though I know it's not and can never be.

Because no one has ever loved me enough to want to keep me.

You're wrong. Katherine did.

But then she was one of a kind. And Edward... he's a very, *very* different kind.

The kind that wields the power to break me so completely if I let him.

CHAPTER FIVE

Edward

MY CAR PULLS up outside her hotel bang on time and I'm surprised to find her already waiting on the pavement. Perched on her backpack, one booted foot tapping, her arms wrapping a vibrant yet ridiculously thin kimono around her.

Does the woman not own a coat?

It's not raining today, but the clear sky offers no protection from the chill, and even with the sun's rays lighting her up on the pavement it can't be enough to warm her.

I leap out of the car before my driver can approach her. 'Get in. It's freezing out here.'

She shoots to her feet, her cheeks radiating the same heat as her eyes. I've annoyed her, but I don't care. Where is her common sense?

'Hello to you too.'

I ignore her snippy remark and grab her bag, handing it to my driver as she gives a huff of protest.

'Get in, Summer,' I repeat, holding open her door. 'As much it will save me a headache or two, I really don't want you to catch your death right now.'

She stares at me hard, opens her mouth and closes it again. Whether it's because of the hint that I might actually care about her wellbeing or the cold itself, she finally moves. Shrugging her satchel off her shoulders and slipping inside, she promptly slams the door in my face.

I look over the roof, take a breath and deny the smirk that wants to form. 'Keep it under control.'

I walk around the car and get in the same side I exited.

'Seatbelt,' I say, without looking at her, knowing she won't have fastened it.

I'm saved from a retort by my driver, who catches her eye in the rear-view mirror, and she gives a soft sigh, does as I've asked. More for his benefit than mine, but that's just fine.

As soon as she's secure he pulls away from the kerb and I breathe more easily…until I catch the faint trace of her perfume. Light, sunny…all her.

'Are you always this grumpy, or do you save it just for me?'

Another smile teases at my lips and I beat it back. This isn't amusing. If I could stay grumpy this wouldn't be such torture.

'Behave like an obstinate child and I'll treat you like one.'

'A *child*? What the—?'

She breaks off as the privacy glass glides into position, saving my driver from hearing more than he should.

'How *dare* you?'

Slowly, I turn to face her. Prepare myself for having her so near. The luxurious back seat is far too cosy, and never have I needed us to be at loggerheads more.

'You're stood outside in the freezing cold, paying no heed to the weather—how else should I treat you?'

'"Paying no heed"?' she splutters back at me, laughing, her eyes wide and disbelieving. 'What century did you walk out of?'

'Cut the attitude, Summer.'

'*My* attitude? Have you checked yourself out in the mirror lately?'

Heat collides with heat. Her chest is undulating so rapidly with her breaths that her kimono parts and my eyes unwittingly dip. I fist my hands against the pulse in my groin and she grunts, tugging the fabric back together and throwing herself back in her seat, arms folded, pout to die for.

'For your information,' she blurts to the passing world outside, 'I don't own a coat.'

'You don't…?' I frown. She can't be serious. 'How can you not own a coat?'

She fires a look at me. 'You want to make a big deal out of that?'

'But Summer—no coat? Seriously?'

'I follow the sun, Edward. I don't *need* a coat.'

'Everyone needs a coat.'

'Not when everything you own has to fit on your back, you don't. I carry what I need. Satisfied?'

Her eyes dare me to object, but I'm already pressing the intercom to speak my driver. 'Parker, we're taking a detour. Miss Evans needs to purchase some clothes.'

'Don't be ridiculous, Edward!' She gapes at me. 'We're not going shopping.'

'We are.'

'Don't we have a train to catch?'

'No.'

'Well, if we're driving the whole way it would be nice to get there before sundown, so... What? Why are you looking at me like that?'

'We're not driving.'

'A bus...?'

She gives me a confused frown and now I really am struggling not to laugh. Me on a bus? Is she serious?

'We're taking the helicopter.'

'The *helicopter*?' she chokes out. 'Are you for *real*?'

I say nothing.

'Of course you are.' Now it's her head that's shaking, her lips twisted in disdain. 'I really shouldn't be surprised, should I?'

'I don't know, Summer,' I say evenly. 'The helipad is a recent addition to the estate. It stands to reason you wouldn't know about it.'

I feel her continued censure as she stares out of the window. What exactly is her problem? The fact that I'm highlighting her absenteeism or the fact that my considerable wealth makes such things as a helipad possible?

Would she be so disgruntled if she knew the reason the helipad exists at all?

I have the ridiculous urge to explain, but bite my tongue. I don't care for her opinion. We just need to get through the next few days, weeks, months—a year, even, heaven forbid—without killing each other.

'Where to, sir?' Parker's voice pipes through the car, reminding me he's waiting for a revised destination.

'Harvey Nicks.' It's the most obvious choice—everything under one roof. Quick. Simple. Efficient.

She looks back at me, her blue eyes bright. 'We are *not*.'

I hold her blazing gaze, unperturbed. 'Would you rather House of Fraser, or—?'

'We're not going shopping, Edward!'

'No, we're not. *You* are.'

'I don't have the money to just—'

'Correction. You do have the money—or have you forgotten already?'

'Seriously, Edward, you're—'

'Sir?' Parker prompts as we approach a set of traffic lights.

'Harvey Nicks. And delay our take-off by two hours, please.'

'Two hours! What on earth are we shopping for that will take two hours?'

'As you've just explained, you have a bag full of summer-wear—or am I mistaken?'

'No, b—'

'Then we're going shopping. You can use my card.'

'I don't want to use your blasted card, Edward,' she erupts, her bottom lip jutting out with her displeasure.

It's so perfectly kissable, I can almost taste it.

'No…' Inside, I curse, battling my impossible reaction to her as I go on the attack. 'You'd rather behave like a petulant child—again.'

Her eyes flash. 'Say that again and I'll—I'll—'

I raise my brows at her. 'You'll what?'

She makes a growling sound and slams back into her seat. 'When did you get so *infuriating*?'

'When you left without a goodbye.'

Idiot! Where did that come from?

I race to fill the silence but she's there first, her voice sickeningly soft, 'Edward, I'm sorry for what—'

'Save it, Summer. I'm not interested in looking back. All I care about right now is ensuring you don't die of hypothermia.'

'I don't need you to sort out my wardrobe.'

'Because you've done such a great job of it yourself?'

She re-wraps her kimono around her, case in point. The flimsy thing in no way up to the task of fending off the Scottish weather…even so, I can't deny that I love it. The vibrant colours. The way it sets off her eyes, her wild hair, the sun-kissed glow of her skin…

But then I'd love anything on her—that's the problem.

What the hell is wrong with me?

'I've not had the time to think about something as simple as my wardrobe. My head's been full of all this since I returned.'

I scan her face, see her sincerity for what it is. 'Have you read your letter now?'

'Yes,' she admits quietly. 'I've read the letter.'

'And?'

'And I too disagree with much of it.'

'Common ground at last.'

She gives a huff-cum-sigh.

'In which case, I assume you'll also agree that we need to find a way around the conditions of the will—specifically those relating to where we live for the next year.'

Her eyes probe mine. 'Why?'

'Are you seriously asking me that?'

Her cheeks flush a delectable shade of pink, her lack of make-up offering up no protection from my watchful eye. She used to go in for heavy eyeliner, pale foundation, subtle blusher… Not that she needed it then—or now. Though I'm sure she'd appreciate its concealing benefits if I told her that her skin gives away her every emotion. Anger. Frustration. Sadness… Desire.

'Do you have somewhere else you need to be for the next year, Edward? Or do you simply want to get away from me?'

My laugh is cold and abrupt as I turn to the window. I don't want her to see the bitterness in my face. I don't want her to know how much it stung when she left.

Her shocking departure cut deeper than the emotional neglect I suffered at the hands of my parents and has affected every relationship I've attempted since.

No one gets to see me that weak. Not any more.

'Want to swap letters?' she murmurs into the quiet, and I flinch.

'Hell, no.'

'Spoilsport,' she mutters under her breath.

Silence descends—heavy, strained—and I count the seconds until I can break out of the car, break free of her...

I've never been more relieved to see the front of a department store. The five-storey building a welcome sight of sandstone, granite and gleaming glass. I leap out as soon as the car pulls up and catch the tail-end of Summer's hushed laughter as I go.

I wait for her on the pavement and she strides straight past me, her words trailing on the chilling breeze. 'I never thought I'd see you so eager to shop, Edward.'

I bite my lip. Me neither.

Oh, Gran, if you could see me now you'd be laughing with her...or maybe that was your intention all along.

Summer

I thought nothing could beat the weird adrenaline rush of shopping with Edward.

At first, I was hesitant. 'Uncooperative', to use his word. But I've never been a girly-girl. I've never had the cash to spare or the friends to shop with. Moving from foster home to foster home, school to school, can do that to you.

But under his undivided attention, hearing his honest opinion on what worked and what didn't, what colours, what styles... I was lapping it up by the end.

It sure beat the animosity tainting our every other interaction up until now...even the one when he'd apologised. Sort of.

And with every compliment he paid my body warmed, and my ego with it. Not that he was flirting, or anything close. He said it like a statement of fact. Like it should be obvious to me what shades brought out the blue of my eyes, the honey in my hair...

It didn't mean anything. But it had been so long since anyone had taken charge with my interests at heart. He *cared* that I didn't catch my death and it felt...it felt good. Dangerously good to let someone care for me on some level and take the lead.

But now I'm here, in his helicopter, of all things, with the Scottish landscape drifting by beneath us. A patchwork quilt of greens, browns and hints of purple. Landbound lochs and rolling hills. Seeing it all from the air is incredible—an adrenaline-packed ride, quite literally.

'If I didn't know any better, I'd say you're enjoying this.'

Edward's voice crackles through my headset and I can't help the smile that's busting my cheeks.

'It is stunning!'

'And yet you've stayed away for so long.'

His sudden attack steals my breath and I look back to the window, hide my guilt, my confusion, my pain. How could he begin to understand how I felt? He was born into his world, Katherine's world, and for all his grandmother tried to make me feel at home she couldn't eradicate the doubt. The doubt that Edward's own mother had picked up on and used against me.

'It was better that way.'

I grip my hands together in my lap. *Better for who?* I feel the dig in my ribs—a sharp, acute pain. *Selfish. Selfish. Selfish.* Protecting myself when I should have been…

But I didn't know she was sick! If I had, I would've moved heaven and earth to be here.

'What? Staying away?' he presses, his disbelief audible. 'Even when Gran was diagnosed…?'

I flex my fingers, breathe through the pain.

'No…' My voice catches as I risk meeting his penetrative gaze. 'Not then.'

'Why, then? Why not come home when you knew she was sick?'

'Because I didn't know.'

I look away in my shame, my guilt, and say it so quietly I'm surprised he hears me over the blades beating loudly above our heads and the static through the headphones.

He leans across the lush cabin—swankier than I ever thought possible in such a confined space— and touches my leg, tries to get my attention.

'What do you mean, you didn't know, Summer?'

'Just what I said…' I swallow the bulging wedge in my throat, blink back the tears. 'She didn't tell me.'

'But all this time you claimed to be in touch. Hell, Charles assured me you'd always been in her life, that her love for you was as strong as it ever had been, that you were close.'

Close? I nip my lip and the tears keep on coming. The retort is on the tip of my tongue. *So close she didn't think to tell me something as important as the fact she was dying.*

But I can't say it. It hurts too much.

'Summer?'

'What, Edward?' I shoot back, my eyes piercing his. I'm angry that he's pressing me on this. Something I haven't been able to come to terms with myself. 'You know what she was like! She didn't want to be seen as weak, as vulnerable, to have people fussing. She wouldn't have wanted me to worry on the other side of the world. She wouldn't have wanted me packing up my life to come back for her. She wouldn't have wanted me…wanted me…'

I fumble for more reasons—reasons that I've told myself a thousand times over. But the only one I truly believe is that she didn't love me enough to think I needed to know…

Or, worse, she thought I didn't love her enough to care.

And if that's the case why the inheritance? Why the letter so heartfelt and full of future promise?

'No, you're right.' He snaps his hand back. The lines bracketing his mouth deepen as he presses his lips together, the rich brown depths of his eyes haunted by his own grief, his own confusion. 'She wouldn't have wanted you to worry or change your life for her.'

I ignore the way his words stick the knife in deeper and ask, 'How long was she sick?'

'I can't believe you didn't know…'

'I didn't, Edward. Please, you *must* believe me on this.' Desperation makes my voice hoarse. 'Do you really think I would have stayed away if I'd known?'

He debates it for longer than I like, his stare intense, and then he blinks and I see the shutters lift, the resignation in his sagging posture.

'She was sick for a while.' He sinks back into his seat, his eyes going to the window, lost in the past. 'Like you say, she didn't want to make a fuss. It was only when she couldn't hide the pain that I forced her to admit something was wrong.'

His voice cracks but he doesn't stop.

'She refused treatment. Said it would only prolong the discomfort, make her feel worse, and she'd prefer to spend her last few months on this earth pretending it wasn't happening...'

He takes a ragged breath and I fight the impulse to reach out for him, to offer comfort that I know he won't welcome.

He turns to look at me. 'You know, I don't think she would have told me either if she could've avoided it.'

He looks so broken, so defeated, and I know what the admission has cost him. Gone is the cold executive. In his place is a glimpse of the man I knew and my heart aches for him.

'She was too independent for her own good,' I say.

'She was too stubborn, you mean.'

'Stubborn, independent—same difference...' I attempt a nonchalant shrug, a sad smile, and I surrender to the need to touch him, to comfort him, to share this moment...especially when I can only guess at how rare it might be. I cover his hand with my own, feel him flinch. But he doesn't break away and I tell him with all the feeling I can muster, 'She loved you, though.'

His eyes reach inside mine, and a thousand

shadows chase across his face. 'It appears she loved us both.'

Did she? 'I guess…'

'You guess?'

I look away from his surprise. Of course he won't understand. How can he when I haven't explained myself? I think back to that God-awful phone call a few weeks ago, when Mr McAllister rang me and informed me of her death. Out of the blue. No warning. Nothing.

'I was so *angry*, Edward. Not when I learned of her death—not then. I was shocked, grief-stricken… But when I learned that she'd been sick, that she'd known she was going to—to—' I swallow down the tears. 'That she didn't have much time left. How could she take away my chance to say goodbye? Why didn't she want me to come back? Why didn't she want me here? I would have come—I would have. She should've known that.'

He covers my hand on his. 'Maybe she didn't want your last words to be filled with pain.'

I drag my eyes back to his. 'Like yours were?'

He nods, and in that moment the bond, the connection, is undeniable. The years fall away without the hurt, the distance, and the defensive walls we've erected since.

'How—how was she?'

'Towards the end?'

I nod, and he surprises me with the smallest of smiles. 'Fierce.'

'Fierce?' I mirror his smile and he nods again.

'Like you wouldn't believe. Mind over matter, they say, and she was that through and through, refusing to bend to the illness. But that last fortnight she shrank. She grew tired. She wanted—she wanted it over.'

'And you were with her?'

'As much as possible. It's the reason for the helipad.'

I frown, and he gestures around us. 'I invested in all this when I found out she was sick. I could get to her quicker...more often.'

And I'd been thinking it was just a way of splashing his cash. I feel a stab of guilt and squeeze his fingers. 'I'm so glad she had you.'

Not just your mother, I want to say, but I don't. I can't imagine she will have changed much in all the years I've been away.

'Me too.'

We fall silent, our eyes connected, the mood in the cabin heavy with our grief, our newfound understanding...

There's so much I want to say. So much I want to do. I want to wrap my arms around him, hold him close, absorb his pain like my own.

'Sir?'

I start as the pilot's voice breaks through the headset.

'We're coming in to land.'

Edward looks at me—a look I can't decipher.

'Thank you, Angus.'

He withdraws from my touch.

'You should check out the view. You've never seen Glenrobin from this angle.'

Slowly, I do as he suggests, my head and heart slow to shift focus. I should be grateful for the timely interruption. Should be, but I'm not.

I look at the ground beneath us and press a palm to my chest, comfort my unsteady heart as I take in the sheer beauty below...

'Something else, isn't she?'

I nod as I take in all that has changed and all that remains the same.

The far-reaching loch with its wooden jetty where I first met Edward. The new addition of what looks to be a boat house. The dense woods that punctuate the skyline and run along one edge, up into the mountains, and the rolling fields where the estate's game roam free. And nestled in the heart of its wild surroundings the majestic house itself.

Glenrobin Castle, in all its austere beauty.

'It's even more breathtaking than I remember.'

'And it's half yours now.'

I can hear the continued disbelief in his tone, his discontentment too, and I feel it through and through. *This can't be mine.*

I gaze along the lawn at the vast baronial building with its château-inspired pepper-pot turrets, all granite and slate and irregular in shape. It has a gothic fairy tale vibe, and if I hadn't lived here once upon a time I'd have a hard time believing such mythical beauty exists. Let alone accepting I own any part of it.

I'm mesmerised as the pilot touches down with a gentle bump, the carefully groomed lawn kicking up dirt and grass as it settles into position.

'It hasn't changed a bit,' I whisper to myself as Edward speaks to the pilot, and I'm surprised to hear him respond.

'Not from the outside, but you should see some improvements to the amenities inside, and there are a few holiday rentals dotted about the land now. It needs renovating in parts, but we're getting there.'

If I'm not mistaken, it's the sound of pride in his voice. Is Edward responsible for it all? Has he been helping to take care of Glenrobin for a while now?

Even more reason for him to resent me and my share.

Not for the first time, I wonder at his parents' lack of involvement, their small by comparison inheritance. Now isn't the time to ask him about it, though. I'm exhausted. It's early evening here, but it's the middle of the night in Kuala Lumpur and I'm still on Malaysian time.

How easily sleep will come is another matter. Being back here…with all the memories I've tried hard to forget, all the feelings I've tried to suppress. Last night was impossible enough, but tonight…in a new bed in a new room in a house I know of old…

Where will I sleep? Do I get to choose? Has Edward chosen for me?

'You ready?' Edward looks to me expectantly, his seatbelt already undone as he gestures to the door that has been opened without my noticing.

I release my belt and clamber forward. My legs feel weak. I want to blame the vibrations of the helicopter, but I know it has more to do with him and the castle I'm walking into—the dawning responsibility of it too.

I grip the handrail as I carefully step down to the ground, my eyes fixed on the house and the staff I can see waiting, though I can't make out their faces. Will I know anyone? Will they remember me? Do they know we're now...? What are we, exactly? Their new employers?

Edward's palm presses into my lower back and I inhale sharply, heat rushing to greet his touch.

'Sorry, I didn't mean to startle you!' he shouts over the helicopter blades. 'But unless you want your ears ringing all night we should move!'

'Oh, right...of course!' I scrape my whipped-up hair back from my face but can't find my legs.

'What is it?' He leans into my immobile form.

'Do they—do they know?'

'About us?'

My eyes shoot to his—*us*? Oh, how I once wished that we could have been just that—an us.

'Summer?'

'About the new ownership!' I blurt. 'The conditions—all of it?'

'Yes, they know enough!'

I nod, but still I'm rooted. There are five people standing in the distance, all in the same navy and white unform, bodies ramrod-straight, hands clasped before them.

'How did they take it?'

'They loved my grandmother and they respect her wishes. That's all you need to know!'

You don't, though, my heart screams as his palm urges me to move.

'Come on! Marie will get tetchy if we're late for dinner!'

'Dinner?' The idea of eating anything feels impossible. But then… 'Hang on, did you say Marie? *Marie* is still here?'

'Yes.'

He smiles now, the closest thing to a genuine smile I've seen him give, and a wave of happiness flows through me. I cling to it, use it to give me the confidence I've been lacking.

'And whatever you do, don't mention retirement to her—not unless you want something akin to gruel for breakfast each day!'

'Thanks for the warning!' I manage to say, happy to know there will be one friendly face at least.

I only wish it could be his.

CHAPTER SIX

Edward

I INTRODUCE SUMMER to the staff, but my eyes are all for her, watching her every move.

She's nervous. The nip she gives her bottom lip between introductions is so very telling, but then she smiles and I watch it work its magic over everyone. She's wearing one of her new sweaters—a chunky knit in fluorescent pink. It should hurt my eyes. Instead it enhances everything about her…everything that seems designed to entice me.

More layers were meant to be a *good* thing. The less flattering and the thicker the better. But I'm staring at her now and I've never wanted her more. Hot off the back of our emotional exchange, our shared grief and understanding… Is it possible to be starved of someone for so long that their appeal returns so much stronger for the deprivation?

Marie lets out a squeal of delight that jolts right through me, saving me from myself.

'Miss Summer! This is the best news, lass!' She tugs Summer in for a hug. 'The best, I tell ye!'

James, our butler, clears his throat. It's a warning to Marie, but she's been here longer than me and no amount of throat-clearing will rein her in.

I tear my gaze away, concentrate on the helicopter being unloaded, her baggage so light even with the addition of all the purchases I insisted she make.

Is that really all she owns? She's made no arrangements, no requests to have anything else shipped…

'Mr Fitzroy, sir?' Mrs McDougall, James's wife, calls for my attention. She's been the Glenrobin housekeeper for a decade now and still I address her by her title. As does every staff member, including her husband. 'Shall I arrange for tea in the sitting room?'

'Please.' I turn to Summer. 'Shall we?'

I nod for her to go ahead, but she waits for me. I tilt my head, questioning her hesitation, and her smile tightens in return. She doesn't want to walk in first.

And now the staff are staring, their curiosity mounting, so I move before we can look any more out of place.

I guess it hasn't been her home in so long returning to it must be strange. Particularly when it's not just a home now. It's a responsibility, a job, an estate that needs managing twenty-four-seven to keep it ticking over. I wonder if she realises that. It's no free ride caring for such a large estate—a two-hundred-year-old one at that—no matter how temporary I hope to make this entire arrangement.

I cross the entrance hall, my shoes clipping the rich wooden floor, and that's when I realise it's only my footsteps I can hear. I turn to find her in the middle of the room, the double-height space dwarfing her form as she stares up at the crystal chandelier and then all around. At the wood-panelled walls, the hunting regalia, the portraits of ancestors gone by…

I want to read her mind. I want to know exactly what she's thinking. Is her head racing with the same questions…? How is this supposed to work? What was Gran playing at? How do I resist the way my body reacts to her at every turn?

OK, so that latter problem is all me…

The staff disperse behind her and we're alone once more.

'Summer?'

Her eyes fall to mine, wide, unsure.

'The sitting room is this way.'

Like she needs the reminder… She might have been gone twenty years but her memory is intact.

Still, she nods as if she doesn't already know, then takes another look around, her eyes landing on the tapestry of the family crest that hangs above the inglenook fireplace. Its dominant presence leaves guests in no doubt as to who this house belongs to…even if Gran has now stuck a dividing line down its middle.

But to Gran, Summer was family. She became family the second she moved in all those years ago.

'Summer?' I try again, and this time she moves,

tucking a loose strand of hair behind her ear and avoiding my eye. 'Are you okay?'

I'm angry at myself for asking. Even more angry that my heart insists on caring.

She gives another nod, but I know she's not. *She* knows she's not. And it should make me happy, but I'm not.

I want to howl with frustration. Instead I clench my jaw shut, don't open it again until we're settled in the sitting room and the tea has been poured. I thank Mrs McDougall and tamp down the desire to ask for something stronger—neat.

'You're welcome.' She pauses on her way out the door. 'Which rooms would you like your luggage in?'

I glance at Summer and she's nipping at her lip again.

'I'd be happy with my old room...' She directs it at me and I shake my head.

'That's not going to work.'

'Why not?'

'Because those rooms haven't been occupied in years—and besides, you are to all intents and purposes the lady of the house now.' I can't hide the bitter tinge to my words. 'You should have Gran's old room.'

She pales. 'No...' she whispers. 'I couldn't.'

It's like a knife twisting inside my chest, her obvious upset, and I want to take it back. The pain I've inflicted. But what of *my* pain? Why can't I fixate on that and use it to protect myself and keep her at arm's length?

'And may I remind you,' she continues on, her voice stronger now, 'that not two days ago you made it clear I would never be seen as—'

'One of us needs to,' I interject quickly, knowing what she's about to say and not wanting Mrs McDougall to bear witness. 'My mother will have the east wing for her visits—for now. And many of the rooms to the rear, including your old one, are in desperate need of renovation.'

'I think what you class as "desperate need" and what I class as "desperate need" are very different. I'm sure my old room will be plenty good enough, Edward.'

Mrs McDougall's eyes are flitting back and forth between us. Her expression is unreadable but she's certainly taking note. I'm not used to being questioned—especially in front of my staff. Coupled with the way Summer's getting under my skin…and in the very house where we share a past… I need this conversation over. *Now.*

'No.' My tone brooks no argument. 'It won't.'

'Fine.' She folds her arms, stares me down. 'But I'm not taking the master suite.'

Mrs McDougall chokes on what definitely sounds like a laugh.

'Fine,' I bite out. 'I'll take the master suite and you'll take the adjoining room.'

Her mouth quirks just a little, and there's no missing the triumphant spark in her eye.

'I trust that is satisfactory?' My voice is as tight as my hand around the delicate china cup.

'Very.' She graces me with a smile so sickly sweet that I want to recoil…or stride across the room and kiss it from her…bury the chaos of this situation in what I know would be explosive. No matter how unwise.

'There you have it, Mrs McDougall. You can prepare the rooms.'

'Absolutely, sir.'

I sip my tea, force my hand to relax, my body too, and listen for the click of the door closing on her exit.

'It would be better if we saved the arguments for behind closed doors,' I say.

Her frown is instant, the smirk on her lips quicker still. 'Edward! Are you serious?'

'I would prefer it if the staff were not aware of our…issues.'

Now she laughs. '*Issues?* Is that what you're calling it?'

'What would you call it?'

'Well, that just now was us discussing sleeping arrangements. I hardly think it's a criminal offence for Mrs McDougall to know that I don't want to sleep in Katherine's room.'

'And what makes you think that I w—?' I snap my mouth shut on the heartfelt admission. Dammit all. Why can't I keep a handle on it when she's around?

She starts to lift out of her seat, her eyes softening as she reaches for me. 'Edward, I'm sorry, I didn't—'

'Leave it, Summer.'

I'm out of my seat faster than her. I don't want to hear it. I'm sick of feeling...like this. I need to get out of her orbit. I need air without her sunny scent. I need space without the sight of her chewing on her luscious lip, without the familiar flecks of gold in her expressive blue eyes, without the sympathy...no more sympathy.

'Now that the bedrooms are sorted, I have some calls to make.' I rise with my cup in hand, although I intend to replace it with something stronger as soon as I'm alone. 'Can you find your own way to yours?'

'I'm sure I'll manage.' But she eyes the doorway as if at any moment it might bite her...

'You don't look sure...'

Her eyes flit to me. 'It's just...it's so strange, being back here. I never thought... Well, I didn't think. And especially not now—not without Katherine.'

Her voice cracks, and for the first time since she arrived I see her grief written in her face. It runs so much deeper now that we're here, surrounded by my grandmother's legacy.

'I know. Her presence is as big as the house itself…her absence too.'

She twists her hands in front of her and I can't take the sight of her all vulnerable and alone.

'Right, I'll take you up.' The words are abrupt with my frustration, and I grimace as she flinches. 'Sorry. I'm tired. I didn't get much sleep last night.'

'You and me both.'

Her fingers tremble as she reaches for her cup and I step in, lifting it for her. We're so close now—too close—and I keep my eyes trained on the door as I wait for her.

Just show her to her room.
Get yourself to yours.
Get the space you need.
Simple.
Or it should be…

Summer

From the safety of the bedroom threshold, Edward points out the access to the dressing room, the bathroom and, with a bob of his prominent Adam's apple, the interconnecting door to his bedroom.

And then he's gone, leaving a hint of his cologne in his wake and a whole heap of tension in the air. I'm not blind to the banked desire behind his eyes, the desire he doesn't want to feel…

Well, join the club!

'Is this what you wanted, Katherine?' I whisper into the room. 'Is this meant to be a gift and a punishment in one?'

I think about the letter. Think about the way I'd sometimes catch her watching us when we were younger, a smile about her lips and a sparkle in her eye. I didn't intentionally give away my feelings—my body did it for me... Something Edward's own mother took great delight in highlighting once upon a time.

My cheeks burn as the memory threatens to engulf me and I'm saved by a knock at the door. I turn to it, press my palms to my cheeks and take a breath, smile. 'Come in.'

James opens the door, his arms heavily laden. 'I have your baggage, Miss Summer.'

My smile falters. 'Please, just call me Summer, James. I feel like I should be looking for my mother when you say "Miss".' And if I don't want to think about Edward's mother, I certainly don't want to be thinking about my own. 'If you wouldn't mind, that is?'

He seems to think about it for a second more and then he straightens, gives a nod. 'Very well... Summer. Can I send for Mrs McDougall to help you unpack?'

He eyes my luggage, specifically my backpack, and his brow furrows. He probably thinks a rat will run out of the worn canvas at any moment. Such a contrast to the crisp white department store bags with their fussy black bows and block letters, all carefully filled to the brim thanks to Edward.

'No, it's fine. I'll take care of it.'

'Of course. Can I get you anything else?'

'I'm fine, thank you, James.'

With another swift nod he leaves me, his pace far steadier than Edward's was.

Now it's just me, my cup of tea and a thousand memories all making themselves known.

Oh, Katherine, you really have done a number on us both.

I walk to the bed, sink into its edge, careful not to spill my drink. The bedding alone looks like it's worth more than the entire contents of my backpack. And don't get me started on the rest of the room…

The exquisite furniture that looks ancient yet pristine. The heavy tartan drapes in front of the large bay window that curves with the turret and offers space to sit and survey the land. The pillows sumptuous and inviting. The tapestry rugs adorning the floor and the gilt-framed paintings of landscapes and people gone by on every wall.

It's yours now…

Like hell it is. None of this is mine.

And yet the legal documents and the letter from Katherine say it is. Half of it, at least.

I suck in a breath…let it out slowly. Take another…

It's time to stop questioning it and do as Katherine says—look to the future and *'forge a bet-ter path to happiness'*. Whatever that means…

I know one thing for certain: looking back isn't going to help us move forward. We need to lay the past to rest, and that means forcing him to hear the apology he doesn't want to listen to.

Mind made up, I unpack, trying to make the room feel like home. I place the photo Katherine gave me as a leaving gift on the bedside table, where it always lives, and Ted beside it. My little bear is so tatty it's a miracle he still has all his limbs. He's the only thing left from my life before foster care and he's travelled everywhere with me.

'Welcome to your new abode, Ted.' I pat his threadbare head.

I'm not sure why I keep him. I'm not even a hundred percent certain he came from my mother. But I guess he's a reminder of where I came from…and he's a warning, too. Not to get attached. That even those who should love you by blood soon realise you're not worth it.

'Not us, though, hey, Ted? We have each other.'

I tackle the dressing room next…or rather it tackles me. My clothes are dwarfed by the sheer size of it. My trainers, walking boots and sandals tuck into one corner, leaving row upon row of va-cant space, the clever lighting accentuating just how bare it still is. And just how ridiculous and out of place I feel using it.

I turn away.

You don't belong here, the empty space whispers at me.

But then Katherine's voice from the past overrides it. *'This is your home for as long as you want it to be, Summer.'*

'Home,' I repeat aloud, testing it for size.

I don't do homes. It's not just people I avoid becoming attached to, but places too. I run before I'm pushed. It's served me well until now...

And I know Katherine insists this isn't emotional blackmail, but I can't help feeling it is—just a little.

'She's a monkey, Ted,' I say, walking back into the bedroom and grabbing up my toiletry bag.

I find the bathroom already stocked as I unpack my own toiletries. I eye the expensive-looking body wash and have the silly urge to sniff it, just to see if it smells of Edward, and snap my hand back to my side—*weirdo!*

It's then I see my reflection in the mirror above the sink and grimace. I look like I've been dragged through a hedge backwards.

Jet-lagged me is bad enough. Jet-lagged me with a disturbed night and a body in turmoil over being back here with Edward is something else. I'm hovering between startled rabbit and Mad Hatter. And don't even get me started on my hair. Do helicopters *do* that?

I check my watch and curse. I have ten minutes to get ready.

I strip swiftly and hit the shower. It's vast, the marble tiles spotless, the jets hot and fierce and everything my aching body needs.

Clean and refreshed, I feel more awake and ready to face the music. To face him.

I choose my clothes carefully. Jeans and a cream fine-knit sweater—one that Edward helped me choose that afternoon.

Edward, Edward, Edward.

I grit my teeth, shake out the taunt. I feel like a teenager mooning over him again.

But I had an excuse back then.

I was young, not quite naive—no child can live through foster care and be that—but foolish enough to believe in real-life fairy tales. He was the first guy to show me the right kind of attention, looking beneath the bad-girl exterior, the cocky arrogance, to the girl beneath. He saw the real me, listened to me, and I let him in…started to care…

'So, the smoking—it's all part of the image, right?'

We'd taken a run up into the mountains, the second summer he'd come home. He'd been determined to get me fitter and I—well, I never could resist seeing him working up a sweat. We'd collapsed against a sunbaked rock, our eyes on the blue sky, our conversation turning deep.

'What makes you say that?'

'Because you rarely roll up any more.'

I'd shrugged. 'I haven't wanted to.'

He'd pushed himself up on one elbow and looked down at me, his hair flopping forward in its sexy habit, and my entire body had thrummed with the possibility that this might be it. Today he might kiss me and fulfil the dream I'd had since the first day I'd met him.

'I think it's more than that...' The sincerity in his chocolate-brown eyes had set my heart racing, my lips bone-dry.

'Oh, you do, do you...?' Husky. Low. I hadn't even sounded like me.

'I think you know you don't need to be like that around me...you don't need the front.'

'No? And why's that?'

'Because I like the person you are beneath the shield, Summer. And you should like her too.'

My laugh had been awkward, cut short by my heart bursting against my ribs as he'd leaned that little bit closer.

'Just remember that, okay...?'

'Oh, how times change,' I say now, into the bathroom mirror.

Now I know better, and I only wish my body would get the message.

I snatch up my mascara, give my lashes a quick sweep, put some gloss on my lips and the slightest hint of blusher. If anything, it'll give me some protection when my cheeks flush, as they inevitably will. I towel-dry my hair and run a brush through it. I don't have time for more.

'It's not like he expects to be dining with the country's finest, so get over yourself,' I mutter, heading for the door and wishing I'd purchased slippers on our impromptu shopping spree.

These big houses are cold at floor level, and even the thickest socks I have aren't seeing out the chill. But wearing my walking boots to the dining room is uncouth even by my standards, and my sneakers are as threadbare as Ted.

So, cold tootsies it is.

I reach for the handle as the sound of the door opening next door reaches me. I pause, press my ear against the wood. Sure enough, I can hear Edward approach and I hold my breath—why, I have no idea. He pauses just outside and I lean back, eye the door as if it might suddenly explode. And then…the footsteps continue on.

A smile plays about my lips. Edward Fitzroy, future Lord, billionaire CEO, confident, revered, desired by the female population, is afraid to call on me for dinner.

Afraid?

You're the one hiding behind the door!

I leap forward and pull it open before the inner laughter can take hold and pad out after him, my sock-clad feet silent against the floor. He hasn't heard me and I don't call attention to myself. I'm too content enjoying the sight of his rear. How can a man look just as delicious from behind as he does from the front...?

He's freshly showered too. There's a tantalising scent on the air—citrus, sandalwood, patchouli, perhaps—and it's all him. He's swapped his suit for dark chinos and a navy sweater. His hair, still damp at the edges, catches the golden light of the chandelier as we walk down the stairs, its layered style making my fingers tingle with the desire to reach out and play.

James is waiting outside the dining room as we approach, and he gives us a respectful nod. 'Mr Fitzroy, Mi— Summer.'

I'm about to greet him when Edward spins before me, the move so rapid I almost leap back. 'Summer! I didn't hear you!'

I give a smile that's laced with guilt...a tiny shrug too. 'You seemed to be lost in thought.'

I wasn't devouring your rear with my eyes... honest!

He rakes a hand through his hair and my fingers burn with envy... Until his eyes trail over me, and then my entire body is burning at the obvious appreciation I spy there.

He clears his throat. 'I was...' Then he gestures at my top, his eyes looking but not looking. 'That sweater was a good choice.'

The burn becomes a low-down ache, acute, needy, and my heart is pulsing with a ridiculous amount of joy...all over a sweater.

'I like it…' and there go my cheeks with their blushing '…thank you.'

A heated silence descends, broken eventually by the clearing of James's throat. His trademark move, I'm discovering. 'I'll let Marie know you're ready.'

Edward nods and I step past him, enter the dining room before I can give any more of myself away.

Inside, the drapes are drawn against the dark outdoors and the wall sconces are set to low, setting off the austere beauty of the wood-panelled walls and antique paintings. The fire is roaring in the grate, flames dancing and giving up a heavenly warmth.

The highly polished table that is big enough for twenty has been set for two at the end closest to the fire, and I breathe the smallest sigh of relief. I half expected to walk in and find a place setting at either end of the table, and then I would have had to make a scene as I shifted them closer.

Not that I *wanted* to be closer to Edward, but I didn't fancy shouting my apology across the lit candelabra and huge arrangement of dishes that are sure to arrive courtesy of Marie.

It's intimate, but preferable to the gulf that exists between Edward and I.

The man himself pulls out a chair for me and my stomach comes alive. I feel as if a colony of ants are having a rave in there and I cover it with my palm, lower myself into my seat, while he takes the chair opposite.

I haven't eaten since this morning in the café, before he arrived, but now I can't imagine eating anything until I get my apology out of the way.

I open my mouth and James walks in, followed by Mrs McDougall and Marie, all carrying several dishes.

'Wine?' Edward asks me.

'Please.'

He gives James a nod and the man puts down the food he's carrying and does the honours. I grab my glass the moment it's full and take a satisfying gulp. Both men eye me, passing judgement I'm sure, but I don't care. I need this.

Just as Edward needs my apology…even if he doesn't want to hear it.

CHAPTER SEVEN

Edward

WE'RE LEFT ALONE PROMPTLY. As though the staff sense the mood in the air and want no part of it.

Save for Marie, who has a sparkle in her eye—a sparkle that reminds me too much of Gran. Had the two been in cahoots? Had Marie known about this arrangement even before we did?

I should ask her, although I'm afraid of hearing more than I've bargained for.

'I think Marie has outdone herself for your benefit.' I scan the table—game pie with all the trimmings. 'I hope you have an appetite.'

Better than mine, at any rate, because I can't find any desire for food past my desire for her… no matter what's wise, what's sensible, what's fair.

'I can't remember the last time I ate anything quite so wholesome,' says Summer.

My huff is stilted with tension. 'That's one word for it.'

She closes her eyes, inhales deeply, and I can't tear my gaze from her look of sheer, unadulterated bliss. 'It smells amazing too.'

Her appreciative murmur tugs my gaze lower, to her lips, her angled chin, her throat…

She *looks* amazing…

I clench the fork I've picked up. 'I'm sure it'll taste even better.'

Eat. For God's sake eat and focus on that. Not her.

But swallowing proves trickier than chewing. Especially when she makes no attempt to eat herself.

'Are you not hungry?' I ask.

'I am. I just…'

'You just?'

She wets her lips, nips the bottom one—I wish she'd stop doing that. The hint of vulnerability is killing me, triggering a protective instinct that should be long since dead.

'I know you don't want to hear this, Edward, but I'm going to say it anyway.'

I take up my wine, every nerve-ending on high alert. 'Hear what?'

'I know you want to leave the past in the past, and I get it. But I can't do that until I've told you how sorry I am.'

The food sits like a boulder in my chest, the wine sloshing on top of it, and I can't seem to swallow, or speak, or do anything but stare into the intensity of her blue eyes and acknowledge that she means it.

Though it's too little, too late.

'I'm sorry I left without saying goodbye.'

'I was at university,' I say carefully, stripping

the emotion from my voice. 'You could hardly swing by.'

It's what I told myself back then.

But that hadn't meant she couldn't call, write an email, send me one of the many postcards she sent Gran.

'No, but I could have told you I was leaving that weekend you were here for the ball.'

My teeth grind...my knuckles flash white around my glass. 'Are you trying to apologise or rub it in?'

She flinches. 'I am sorry.'

I hear her. I feel her. But the anger I've been suppressing overflows like a shaken champagne bottle with the cork shot off.

'Why be sorry? My parents often came and went without so much as a hello, let alone a good-bye, so why would it matter that you treated me the same?'

She pales in the candlelight, her gasp barely audible. 'I'm not—I didn't...'

'You didn't think it was the same? That I wouldn't be accustomed to it?'

'Edward...'

She wets her lips. Her fingers reach across the table but I ignore them. I also ignore the pained look in her eyes and press on.

'Or maybe it never even occurred to you? I'm not sure which is worse—to know me as well as you did, to know of my estranged relationship with my parents like you did, and then to walk away without it even occurring to you…'

Her eyes are wide, her shock so very evident that I have my answer, and it cripples me inside. 'Just leave it, Summer.'

'But I— God, Edward, I'm so sorry. I'd never… I'm nothing like your parents.'

'I'll be honest: I expected more from you. I was foolish enough to think—'

No, don't go there. It doesn't pay to bring it up now, when Gran's intentions are so bloody obvious she might as well have employed a matchmaking agency to stand over us.

'But you're right. It doesn't pay to dwell on it. The past is the past.'

'You don't understand, Edward. I couldn't say goodbye to you. It's not because I didn't care, or that I didn't want to, I just… I couldn't. I've never been good at goodbyes, and saying goodbye to you back then…'

She stops talking, and for the briefest of seconds I see a glimpse of the girl she was. Confident and carefree on the surface…broken and afraid underneath.

'I just couldn't do it.'

My jaw throbs. I want to ask her why. I want to demand a reason that will justify the pain she inflicted. But I'm not that twenty-two-year-old desperate for answers any more. I'm past all that—*I am*. And raking over it is only going to confuse the here and now.

Make you vulnerable to her again, you mean.

'Apology accepted.'

She stares at me. 'Is it, though? You don't sound like—'

'I'm a man of my word, Summer. If I say it is, then it is.'

She nods, but her doubt is as obvious as her eyes are blue. Hell, maybe I'm not so sure myself.

But I *want* to accept her apology.

I *want* to not care about any of it any more.

Because caring about it is one step away from caring about her all over again. And I won't go there. I won't.

'I hadn't—I never even thought about your parents…' she admits softly. 'How my leaving might have…' She shakes her head. 'I was so focused on how I felt I didn't…'

'I said leave it, Summer.' Her sympathy is crushing me, tearing me apart. 'Now eat—before it goes cold.'

She doesn't move.

'Look, it's done with. You've apologised. Now eat, Summer. Please.'

She gives me a hesitant smile, clearly wanting to believe my words as much as I do myself. 'Yes, boss.'

My heart flips over. She used to call me that back when we were friends. My habit for taking charge colliding with her own and sparking the cheeky little phrase. I ache over the memory, ache over what we've lost…

'For what it's worth, Edward, I am deeply sorry. And believe it or not I am grateful to Katherine. Not for the inheritance,' she's quick to clarify. 'I know I don't deserve that.'

I exhale softly. No, she doesn't. Only…

Summer's worldly goods dance before my eyes. Her life is so very temporary, and the pang in my chest is undeniable. All those years ago she acted like she was happy being a lone wolf, desperate to get out into the big, bad world. But I was convinced otherwise.

And didn't Gran's letter suggest she'd believed the same. That deep down what Summer truly wanted was a home…somewhere to feel safe, secure…loved.

'I'm grateful to her because she brought us back together, Edward, and no matter what happens I'm glad to see you again.'

The pang in my chest deepens exponentially, my defences pitiful in the face of her honesty. Because she means it—I know she does. And I hurry to release the wine glass before the thing shatters in my grasp.

'Don't worry, I'm not expecting you to feel the same way,' she says, racing to fill the silence. 'I just had to tell you before I could even contemplate enjoying this.'

Finally, *finally* she lifts her cutlery, signalling the end of her confession, but I can't move past the chaos she's kicked up inside.

I should say something. Anything. She's apologised, told me she's glad to see me again, but what can I say?

There's no response capable of summing up how I feel.

I'm not even sure how I feel.

I try to follow her lead and eat, but I can't taste anything. I focus on what I do know—Gran's intention to give Summer a home after so many years of traveling.

Not just Summer, my mind intrudes.

Gran saw it in me too. All the travelling, all the work, never putting down roots. But I tested the waters once, knowing in my gut that it wasn't what I wanted, and I had a lucky escape. Now...

What do I want? What does *she* want?

Do our lives really need fixing? Is Gran right on some level?

'Where have you been the last twenty years?' I ask.

She shrugs as she swallows down her food. 'Where *haven't* I been might be the easier question to answer.'

'Always on the move?'

'Always.'

'So, where do you consider home to be? If you had to choose...?'

She cocks her head to one side. 'Home?'

'Before now, obviously…' Because we're home now—*our home*—until my lawyers determine otherwise, and I can't forget that.

'What's that song? "Wherever I Lay my Hat, That's my Home"?'

A smile teases at my lips. 'Good old Marvin Gaye. It was one of Gran's favourites.'

She smiles with me, her eyes misting over and making the blue depths shine ever brighter. 'It was, wasn't it? I guess it kind of stuck with me.'

I imagine her on trek after trek, adventure after adventure, her eyes alive with the wonder of the world, no responsibilities, the world her oyster… it doesn't sound so bad.

'I assume it makes you happy, living that way…?'

Another shrug. 'I don't like to put down roots. I get angsty if I'm one place for too long.'

'Is that what happened all those years ago? You got "angsty"?'

It's out before I can stop it and I curse my wild tongue.

'It—it was more complicated than that.'

Complicated by her past, I know—I get that. But what about now? What of the future and Gran's wishes? How long before she gets 'angsty' and bails anyway?

'I was eighteen,' she says. 'Katherine had done everything she'd promised, taking care of me until

I was old enough to take care of myself. It was time for me to go.'

'For the lone wolf to leave and find her place in the world…'

She frowns at me, her eyes lost in the past. 'You used to call me that…'

'I used to call you that when I was calling out the front you put on.'

She swallows, her throat bobbing as her chin tilts up. 'Maybe it wasn't a front.'

'Maybe…'

But it's so soft she knows there's no agreement in it.

'And how's *your* front these days?' she asks.

A wry smile touches my lips. Sparring with her is too much fun. Even if it does take me back twenty years, to this very room, collapsed on the rug before the fire after a day of Christmas-present-collecting for the local children's home.

'I'm not the only one with a front…'

The flickering light from the fire had danced in her eyes as she'd wrapped the throw she'd snaffled from her bedroom around our shoulders.

'You're just as bad.'

'Really? How so?'

'You play the prodigal son for your parents—perfect grades, perfect clothes, perfect friends… You laugh more when you're with me, though.'

She'd been teasing me with the last but she'd

been right. I'd spent my entire childhood skirting around my parents, trying to get their attention, being on my best behaviour, coming top of the class, top of the sports field too, bringing home the right friends—the ones with the most influential parents. Anything to get a scrap of attention. To feel an inkling of the love I saw my friends receive in abundance. The kind of love Gran had dished out in spades.

Twenty-two and nothing had changed. I'd still been the dutiful son, working hard, networking... playing the part.

'Ever think you would be happier just being you?' she'd asked.

'I could ask you the same.'

'Maybe we should just run away and be ourselves together.'

I'd laughed, but it had caught in my throat, the very possibility of it. No longer a dream but reality. My parents would lose it entirely, and the idea had only served to make my smile widen.

If only she'd been serious in her offer...

'You need to give up smoking first.'

She'd laughed, but cuddled in closer. 'I haven't smoked a cigarette since the summer.'

'Really? You didn't say.'

'I was saving it for Christmas since it seemed like a big deal to you.'

'You were going to gift me your improved health for Christmas?'

'Pretty corny, eh?' She'd looked up at me, her head resting on my shoulder as she'd given the smallest of shrugs. 'But I thought it would make you happy.'

Kiss her. Kiss her now. Tell her how you feel.

And cross a line? Take advantage? She's barely eighteen and more vulnerable than she'll ever admit.

I'd tugged my gaze from her appeal, looked to the fire.

'Yeah, you're right.' I'd forced a laugh as I'd pulled her in close. 'Pretty corny...but it makes me happy all the same.'

I drag my mind back to the present, to her expectant face dancing in the flames. To the lines around her eyes and her mouth that hadn't existed before. They give her a maturity that lacks the vulnerability of old. Is that why I want her more than ever?

'I don't need a front, Summer. I haven't for a long time.'

'Your parents finally take notice of you?'

The wry smile returns. 'I stopped needing them too.'

She searches my gaze. 'Did you decide their love wasn't worth the effort?'

Is she thinking about her own love too? Now that she knows I tarred her with the same brush?

'No love is,' I say simply. 'Save for Gran's and she's now gone.'

She falls silent. One beat. Two. So many questions race behind her eyes and then, 'You never needed a front for Gran…or me.'

My throat threatens to close over. No, what we shared was effortless. But at least my parents stuck around. Their love may be superficial at best, cruel at worst, but *they* didn't disappear into the night, never to return…until now.

And she's only here now because of Gran.

I need to remember that.

I need to cling to it.

'So…' I sip my wine, use it to ease the discomfort in my chest.

'So?'

Her brows nudge skyward, and there's an edginess to her gaze now as she waits for me to finish what I started.

'You must meet a lot of people on your travels.'

'I do.'

'You must make a lot of friends.'

She tilts her head. 'Some, but I prefer to travel alone.'

I nod, ignoring the way her confirmation reassures me. 'Doesn't it get lonely—no permanent base, no travel buddies?'

She laughs now. 'I'm a grown woman, Edward, I don't need travel buddies.'

No, she's never needed anyone, she told you that over and over.

'And besides, I have plenty of social interaction.

There are the people I meet on my travels—people interested in the culture, the food, the excitement of a new country…'

'Of course.' Though I don't believe for a second that those people can be considered a healthy substitution for real friends.

'And I have followers too—people who are interested in my journey and vice versa.'

'Followers?'

'Yes, you know…social media?'

She's on the defensive now. I can tell by her rigid posture, and her cheeks blazing as deep as her eyes.

'You know—that internet thing that everyone uses.'

'Not quite everyone.'

'Well, not you, obviously.' There's a hint of disdain in her voice. 'Far be it for you to lower yourself to the standard of the masses.'

'What's that supposed to mean?'

'Nothing.'

'It's not nothing.'

Her chin is back at its defiant angle. 'I made the mistake of forgetting who you are for a second.'

There's something more than challenge in her eyes—something dangerous and taunting—and it runs deeper than this moment here and now.

'Never mind all this talk of me being lonely— what happened to you?' she fires at me. 'Last I knew you were engaged to be married…quite the match, by all accounts.'

I should have expected it…but it hadn't occurred to me that she would know, let alone raise it now.

'That was a long time ago.' Ten years, to be precise. 'Did Gran tell you?'

'No…' She takes a sip of wine, visibly calming herself. 'I got it from the press.'

'You kept tabs on me?'

The colour reaching up her neck, deepening in her cheeks, is answer enough, and I shouldn't feel the rush of satisfaction, or let the unbidden smile touch my lips.

'What happened?' she presses, avoiding my question.

'My mother happened.'

'She didn't approve?'

'Oh, no—she approved. More than approved. Behind the scenes she was one step ahead of me.'

Her eyes narrow with her confusion. 'What's that supposed to mean?'

'It means Analise was handpicked by my mother. I think she figured that holding the puppet strings over my wife would ultimately keep her hold over me.'

'You're joking!'

She palms her chest as her wine catches in her throat. Far more disturbed than I am. But this is ancient history. I can talk about it without a shred of regret…unlike our situation.

'Seriously, Edward!'

'I am serious.'

She coughs. 'But when did you—*how* did you find out?'

'I came home early from a business trip. I wanted to surprise Analise…' The slightest burn of humiliation reaches my cheeks as I remember *that* particular scene. 'Instead, she surprised me.'

'She did?'

'I found her in bed with our gardener.'

'What?'

'Such a cliché, right?'

'Edward…' She shakes her head, sympathy creeping back into her eyes that I truly don't need. 'I'm so sorry.'

'I'm not. It was a relief to be off the hook—to learn the truth before it was too late.'

'But your mother…what part did she play?'

'Analise came out with all. We had a blazing row. She accused me of being a workaholic, said that she was bored, that she only ever agreed to marry me to keep my mother happy and because my mother had promised she would get her every wish fulfilled. She was moulding her into the perfect daughter-in-law—she was moulding her into herself.'

She gives a dramatic shudder. 'Married to your own mother…heaven forbid.'

A laugh erupts out of me. 'You never were her biggest fan.'

'She was never mine.'

Her voice is stripped of any warmth and there's a glint in her eye that I can't read.

'Don't take it to heart. There aren't many who secure her particular brand of approval.'

'No, I guess not.'

Though it's so quiet I struggle to hear her and I feel like I've lost her somewhere, that her head is in another place, another time. Her eyes... Are those...*tears*?

I lean forward but she looks away, reaches for her glass. She's evading me. Or am I just imagining it?

'Your mother hasn't changed much, then?'

She blinks, her eyes returning to mine tear-free, and it takes me a second to adjust, another to absorb her question. 'Not really.'

She gives a soft huff around her glass, takes a considered sip. 'And there I was, thinking we're supposed to grow as we get older, learn through our life experiences, become better people... Does she know about the inheritance?'

My jaw pulses as I fend off the memory of that particular phone call and nod.

'How did she take it?'

'About as well as you'd expect.'

'Which is...?'

'She threatened to bring in her lawyers, have it contested.'

'You don't seem worried?'

'I'm not.'

'So, you don't think she will succeed?'

'No. Gran did nothing wrong and followed the law to the letter. Charles made sure of that.'

'Yet, you said—'

'I know what I said, but my lawyers are better than hers.'

Are you serious? I cringe on the inside. *How playground do you want to sound?*

Her blue eyes dance back at me and I know she's thinking the same.

'It's the truth,' I swiftly add, which only makes her eyes dance more. 'Hell will freeze over before my mother gets any more of Gran's wealth— movable or otherwise.'

'"Movable or otherwise"?' She frowns.

'It's a legal definition. Things are classified as movable or immovable. In Scottish law you can't disinherit your own children as far as the movable assets go.'

'So, you're saying Katherine had no choice but to give her something?'

'Exactly.'

'But not Glenrobin…the castle, the land…?'

'If I'm honest, I'm not sure Gran would have left her anything by choice.'

'Really?'

'Really, what?'

'Katherine never wrote her off in life—why do you think she'd do such a thing in death?'

I shrug. 'Gran spent her entire adult life trying

to make up for the way things had been when my mother was a child. Perhaps this was a last-ditch attempt at making her see the error of her ways.'

She scoffs, the chip on her shoulder coming to the fore. 'Like she had such a tough time of it.'

'You haven't changed your tune.'

She gives a harsh laugh. 'Edward. Your mother wasn't abandoned or rejected; she was spoilt rotten. Everything she wanted she got. Katherine told me how hard she tried to make up for her lack of a father and getting pregnant so young…how hard she tried to protect her from the disappointment that rained down on them from her high society parents. She forgave her everything.'

'But money and indulgence don't make up for love…'

And isn't that what Gran is trying to tell me in her letter? For all the money I've earned, the success I've achieved in business, none of it has brought contentment, true happiness.

'Katherine *loved* her.'

There's a vehemence to her tone, and I hold her gaze as I tell her the truth Gran once told me. 'She didn't know how to love her—not back when she was a child, during all those influential years that shaped her into who she became. Gran was fifteen when my mother was born. Scared and emotionally cut off from her parents. All she had was their money—and she showered her daughter with it.'

'She showered her with love too. She always cared. Unlike…'

She looks away, her eyes going to the fire as she loses herself in her own thoughts. Her own past. Her own childhood. A mother who didn't fight to keep her…didn't want her, even.

'She could have done a lot worse than having Katherine for a mother.'

'On that we agree.'

My tone is gruff as I read her every thought and feel her pain like a fresh wound. A wound I want to heal even though it isn't my place—not any more. And she wouldn't want me to either. The only person capable of healing her is herself. That was what she always said and what she still stands by now, I'm sure.

'But who knows? Maybe Gran was right to cut her off now. Maybe it will make her question her life choices and have something of an epiphany.'

Her laugh is hollow. 'Do you truly believe that?'

'I can hope. My relationship with my father has improved over the years…maybe there's hope for my mother yet.'

A slow smile builds on her lips, and her eyes start to sparkle. 'Have you become an optimist in your old age?'

'Ha! Less of the old.' But I'm smiling, the sudden lightness far more preferable to the severity that preceded it. 'And, no, I wouldn't go that far.'

'Happy, then?'

'Hmm?'

'If not an optimist, are you happy, at least?'

I stare back at her for a long moment, surprised by her probing question and the way I feel like she should already know the answer…but then how can she? We don't know each other any more.

'I've achieved what I set out to in business. I dominate the industry. I work for my own satisfaction. I do what I want, when I want. When the only person you can disappoint or be disappointed by is yourself, life becomes much simpler. Don't you think?'

'Simple and straightforward…' she reaffirms for me. 'There's a definite truth to that.'

'And you? Are you happy?'

Her lashes flutter. There's a subtle dance flickering in the depths of her eyes—or is it just the flames of the fire…the candles…?

'I'd like to think so.'

She's not sure, though. There's too much hesitation, too much thought.

'There's been no one else since Analise, then? No one serious?'

I straighten. Maybe I should have expected her to dig deeper into my personal life, to push back, and the answer is simple enough, so why I don't give it to her straight is beyond me.

Liar.

'According to the press, there have been many…'

'But according to you…?'

'No, Summer.' I meet her eye, take up my cutlery and stab at my food.

There's been no one because you broke me. Analise didn't even fracture the surface because there was nothing left to break.

'I had a narrow escape,' I permit myself to admit. 'And I have been grateful for it ever since. My life is my own and I prefer it that way.'

She nods slowly, and I think she's about to leave it alone...but then, when did Summer ever leave me in peace?

'What happened to all your dreams of getting married, Edward? Of having children?'

I'm so relieved that my fork hasn't quite made it to my mouth. 'They were the dreams of an inexperienced foolish youth.'

'But what happens to your gran's legacy if you don't marry and have children?'

'I don't know, Summer. You tell me, since it's a problem we now face together.'

She opens her mouth, closes it again, her frown turning her delectable lips down...lips I really don't want to be focusing on...

But has she not even considered it? The future implications of Gran's wishes and how bound together we are now?

'So it is...' she murmurs.

So it is...

No fight, no clever retort, no denial...

As if you really want one.

CHAPTER EIGHT

Summer

I'M STANDING IN *the corner of the Glenrobin ball-room. Around me there are people. So many people. I didn't want to come but Katherine insisted.*

'You're family. You belong here just as much as the others.'

Only belonging can't be handed over. It's a feeling, and I don't have it.

I see the other foster children, so much younger than me, running around the room, enjoying the Christmas festivities that are in full swing. They're not old enough to know better. They've not lived through the disappointment of many Christmases past.

But it's fine. I'm no fool. And, at eighteen, I've decided this is my last Christmas in someone's care. I'll be going it alone. Independent. An adult at last. No more being tossed about in the system. But before I go...

I drag in a breath and scan the room. Edward is here somewhere...the chaotic beat of my heart tells me so...but where?

I spy his companion first. She's impossible to miss. Glossy blonde hair, pinned up in a style that must have taken hours to perfect, her English rose complexion utterly flawless. Her festive red gown fitting her body like a second skin. She's all elegance and poise, oozing money and glamour and everything I'm not.

And she has Edward enraptured.

I fancy he looks at me like that too, with his eyes alive, a charge in the air, a flurry of excitement within him. Is that how it is for this girl too? Have I tried to see more where there isn't more to see?

'She is a vision, is she not?'

I spin on my heel and come face to face with Edward's mother...or Bitchface as I've nicknamed her. Never has there been a woman so beautiful and so sullen in one. A woman who has everything but it's never enough. And don't get me started on how she treats Katherine—her mother by blood, my temporary mother by paperwork.

I refuse to recoil, though every muscle in my body urges me to do so. My skin is crawling under her insipid smile, her hollow cheeks and ice-blue eyes.

Don't get me wrong. She's beautiful...if cool sophistication and high maintenance are your thing. So very different from her son and the warmth he emanates.

'Who?' I say.

She gives a high-pitched laugh and I can't suppress my wince.

'Why, Charlotte, my dear.' She gestures to where I'd just been staring. 'Edward's new girlfriend.'

I must truly flinch now, because she laughs some more, her bony hand fluttering to her neck.

'Oh, foolish child...you didn't think he'd set his sights on you, did you?'

I frown. She's always been a nasty piece of work, but this...this is something else. I want to run, but I don't. I stand straighter. In her three-inch heels she has me on height, but I tilt my chin. I won't cower.

'You don't know what you're talking about.'

'Don't I? Come, now...'

She leans into me, almost conspiratorially. Her sickly-sweet perfume swamps me and I want to gag, cover my mouth, but I won't. I won't be seen as weak in front of her.

'You must think I was born yesterday. I see the way you look at him, with those big blue eyes and that besotted smile. Do you really think you could keep a man like him?'

'I don't think—'

Another cackle of laughter cuts me off and my fingers tighten around the champagne flute Katherine gave me earlier. The glass is still full, and warm now in my hot, sweaty palm. My stomach swoops and my eyes dart about the room.

Is it that obvious? Am I that obvious? Is everyone laughing at me, just as she is?

My cheeks are aflame and I can't quite catch my breath. Does he know? Edward?

'Oh, my dear, I actually feel sorry for you.' She

shakes her head. 'I blame my mother entirely, of course...putting foolish notions in your head. Still, at least you can see the truth for yourself now, before any real damage is done.'

The truth. The same truth I've been trying to keep in mind for the past eighteen months. But instead I've let Katherine and Edward get inside my head...and my heart. I was fine before—just fine. I didn't need them. I didn't need this world where I could never belong.

Charlotte is laughing now. Her whole demeanour reminding me of his mother. My stomach rolls, my heart aches, tears prick...

Oh, God, not here...not here.

'You don't know what you're talking about,' I repeat, trying to move past her.

But my movements are too quick and my glass collides with her. Champagne runs down her front and she lets out a yelp.

'You silly girl!'

'I'm sorry... I'm sorry... I'm so sorry.'

And I'm running—running so fast I can't draw breath. I can't feel the ground beneath my feet. I can't see past the tears, the burn...

I squeeze my eyes shut, open them again, and I'm in a cold, narrow corridor. Ted is in my hand and a woman is walking away from me. A woman I love. A woman I have done everything to try and keep.

'Mummy! Mummy!'

She doesn't turn and I clutch Ted tighter.

It's not my mother any more. It's Edward. Edward walking away.

'Edward!' I choke on the pain, the anguish. 'Edward!'

He doesn't react. His pace is slow and steady, unbreaking, but I can't make my feet go after him.

'Edward!'

He disappears. Just like Mum. He doesn't care. He doesn't want me...

'Summer.'

My name is faint, far away.

'Summer.'

I shake my head, feel softness all around me, an inviting warmth...

'Summer, wake up.'

It's a nice voice. Hushed, husky, deep. There's a hand on my shoulder, gently shaking. A familiar, comforting scent in the air. My eyes flutter open and I squint against the subtle light of the room. Where am I? Who...?

Rich brown eyes come into focus—'Edward!'

I scramble back against the headboard, clutch a hand to my pounding chest, my dream and reality colliding in one.

'Sorry, I didn't mean to startle you...'

I glance around the room. The door between our bedrooms is open. I can see his bed in the distance, the quilt thrown off as though he's left it in a hurry.

Did I scream? Did I…?

My eyes return to his, the dregs of my dream still pulsing through my veins… If only it was purely a dream and not a reminder of the past—of that scene in this house, of my mother walking away many years before…

I used to have it often, but it's not hounded me in years, and I know our conversation over dinner and my return to this place—to him—are to blame.

'Sorry,' he says again. He's perched on the edge of my bed, his hand now resting on the quilt between us. 'You sounded distressed.'

'I did?' Oh, God, what did I say? Should I ask him outright? Did I scream his mother's name or, worse, *his*?

He looks so concerned, his brow furrowed, the wrinkles that have formed over the years only adding to his appeal, and those eyes… *God*, those eyes… I could lose myself in them a million times over and still come back for more.

'Let me get you some water…'

He's rising, but I don't want water.

I don't want to trouble him more than I already have.

I also need him out of here. Because this room, the soft light, his concern, *the bed*—it's all too intimate. And I don't trust myself not to act on what's been virtually a life-long dream…a fantasy. One that could so easily become real in the sleepy confines of this room, at this late hour.

'It's okay, Edward,' I say. 'I don't—'

But he's not listening. He's already heading to the bathroom. And that's when I realise he's wearing nothing but underwear. Tight black briefs that cling to his honed behind, accentuate his trim waist and his muscular thighs with their smattering of dark hair...

The sight steals my voice, my breath...he's so *toned*. Like...*everywhere*.

Heat ripples through my body. My nipples are beading beneath my ancient grey tee. *Oh, God.* It's one thing for him to hear me begging for him in my sleep, but to be all pert and alert and blatantly wanton when awake... No, no, no.

I pull the quilt to my chin just as he emerges, a filled glass in one hand, the other raking through his hair. The thick strands are all mussed up and his face is flushed from sleep. The soft light plays over the chiselled angle of his cheekbones, his jaw, the taut muscles of his chest, the dappled hair that darkens as it disappears into his briefs...

Breathe, Summer.

But he's a vision, a sexual fantasy come to life, and I'm... I'm a hot mess!

'Here.' He offers the glass, his eyes probing mine, his mouth twisted into a one-sided smile.

'Thank you,' I manage to rasp out as I take it. 'I'm sorry I woke you.'

'Don't be. I'm just glad you're not being murdered in your sleep.'

I wince up at him. 'Was I that bad?'

'Put it this way: if it had gone on much longer you would have had the entire household rushing to aid you with any weapon they could find.'

'Oh, dear…'

I wet my lips and realise they taste of salt. My cheeks are clammy too. Was I crying? I swipe the back of my hand over my face, sweep away the hair that's stuck there. Definitely crying. Definitely humiliating.

I sip the cool water, hoping it will ease the rising heat inside me. I'd like to say it's all down to embarrassment, but the fever swirling through my middle is all for him. The throbbing ache too.

I press my thighs together, bring my knees to my chest. I don't look at him as I say, 'I'll be okay now…thank you.'

I bring the glass back to my lips, sip it like a good girl, hoping he'll get the message.

'You sure?'

His scent is carried on the air, the warmth of his naked body too, and my eyes are drawn back to him. The crease between his brows deepens as I blink up at him. His eyes are so dark in the low light.

Am I okay? Right now? Hell, no.

I want to jump his bones. Every nerve-ending is urging me to reach up and pull him to me, to feel those lips against my own. They're so perfect, so full, and his stubble looks tantalisingly rough, his hair wild now it lacks the care he puts into it each morning…

'Summer?'

I snap my eyes back to his, plaster on a smile. 'I'm much better than I was, thanks to you.'

He studies me intently for a second longer than is comfortable and I feel my smile slip. What would he say if I asked him to come to bed with me? As two consenting adults, beholden to no one. No divide. No promises. No lies. Just this…

If I was dreaming, I'd do it.

But this is reality, and it's reality I need to get hold of.

He reaches out and my breath stalls in my lungs. His fingers close around my glass as he slips it from my weakened grasp. 'You're trembling.'

'I am…?' I look down at my fingers and sure enough they're unsteady. But it's more to do with the wild energy now pulsing through me in the aftermath of my dream, my wild fantasy too. 'It'll pass.'

He places the glass on the bedside table and the photo catches his eye. He smiles. 'I remember when that was taken.'

I look at the picture, let memories dance to the fore… 'It was a lovely day.'

'You and Gran had taken the kids pumpkin-picking.'

'And you'd refused—said it was for youngsters.'

He shrugs. 'Gran still roped me in, though.'

'Because she played on your macho instincts.'

His laugh is gruff. '"You can't expect us girls to carry all the big ones…"' He mimics his grandmother, his voice as soft as his expression.

'Well, they were rather heavy—especially the one we used for the carriage.'

'Ah, yes—that scene for the Halloween Fairy Tale Ball.'

'It was Katherine's favourite event of the year.'

'That and Christmas.'

We both stare at the picture, remembering the woman with the huge heart and feeling the massive imprint she's left on our own.

'I miss her.'

The quiet confession falls from his lips and I put my own insecurities aside to reach for his hand, squeeze it softly.

'Me too. She was an incredible woman.'

His eyes lift to mine and I can't breathe, seeing the obvious pain there, the pain that's now morphing into something else. Something heated and desperate. I feel the fire unfurl deep within me, my fingers burning around his. I wet my lips, search for something to say—something that isn't *Kiss me*.

This connection is about grief. Nothing else. Nothing more.

'I should go,' he says.

I nod. He *should* go. I can already feel the boundaries between us blurring. Our lives entwining. It's too easy to forget how different we are. That this is the world in which he belongs. I'll always be on the outskirts looking in, no matter what Katherine wanted otherwise.

He lets go of my hand, starts to walk away.

'Edward?'

He pauses, looks at me over his shoulder.

'I know you don't think I deserve all this—the inheritance, the castle, the estate…'

'That's not—'

I raise my hand, shake my head, cutting off the denial he doesn't need to give.

'I *know* I don't deserve it. But it's an opportunity I don't want to waste. It's an opportunity for me to do so much good—the kind of good Katherine did…'

'What are you saying?'

'I'm saying…' I lift my chin a fraction, uncaring that the quilt has fallen to my waist and that his eyes flit down, resting for a second too long. 'Give me a chance to prove myself to you.'

'You don't need to prove yourself to me.'

'Don't I?'

He hesitates, but I see the answer in his eyes and I can't blame him. With parents like his, his ex-fiancée, people who want him for his wealth and status, not to mention what I did, he's bound to mistrust me.

'Whatever the case, you're a busy man. You have a company that occupies you full-time and I sense you've been running this place for a while too. I don't have the same responsibilities, but I do have the freedom and the desire to carry on Katherine's legacy…help children like I once was.'

He faces me head-on, his brow furrowed once more, and that naked torso is on full display as he folds his arms and his biceps bulge—

Focus, Summer! Eyes up!

'You mean fostering?'

'No… No. I know I'm not in the right place for that—not yet.'

Though never say never…

It's not something I've ever considered—not with how transient my life has been. But aren't things different now…? Might it be an option… one day?

'Then how?' he asks.

One step at a time, I tell myself.

'By giving back to the local community. Volunteering. Carrying on the fundraising events she used to run.'

'Like the Halloween Fairy Tale Ball?'

I smile. 'Yes, like the Halloween Fairy Tale Ball.'

He nods.

'You agree?'

'It's an idea…although it's a lot of work—organising such affairs, I mean.'

'I'm not afraid of hard work, Edward.'

'No, I don't suppose you are.'

He stares at me and I wish I could see inside his

head…see whatever thought it is causing his eyes to shine back at me. I like that look. I want more of that look. It makes my heart skip, my body warm.

And, oh, God, there you go again. Boundaries— you need boundaries.

'Goodnight, Summer.'

He starts to move off and I stall him again. 'Edward?'

'Yes?'

Nerves almost get the better of me, but I clench my fists. This is important. I need to draw a line in the sand and make it clear—for my benefit as much as his.

'This house is big enough for the two of us to live our lives, yes?'

'Yes.' It's part-impatience, part-resignation.

'And just because I'm here, you shouldn't feel like you can't…you can't bring people back.'

I see his surprise in the flaring of his eyes and bite my lip.

'You mean *women*?'

My cheeks burn but I hold my ground. 'I mean anyone—but, yes, women too.'

His eyes dance in the lamplight and I suck in my cheeks. He's laughing at me.

'Are you giving me permission to date, Summer?'

'No. I'm saying that just because we're stuck together for a year it doesn't mean…it doesn't mean we need to put our lives on hold.'

'Our *sex* lives?'

I nod, swallow, squeak—oh, God, did he hear that?

'Believe me, Summer…' His eyes darken, and colour slashes his cheeks. 'If I want to bring a woman home, I will.'

Well, you deserved that.

And then he's gone, and my legs twitch with the desire to run after him, jump him, kiss him, until the only woman he could possibly want to bring home is me.

Edward

I close the door between us, deliberately slow. I don't want her to know that every sinew in my body is straining to go to her, to prove that the only woman I want to bring home is already here.

The moment I heard her scream my name, I shot out of bed. Racing to her side with no thought as to how I was dressed…no thought as to how she would be dressed either.

Such a fool.

I drag a hand over my face, lean back against the solid door and suck in a breath that's no longer tainted with her scent. How can twenty years have gone by and she still possess the same smell? It's driving me crazy. As is her voice, her smile, her laugh…

Hearing her distress, seeing her twisted up

in the bedsheets, her hair clinging to her damp brow… Nothing could have prevented me from going to her side. But the second she saw me and scurried back I knew I'd made an epic mistake.

The way her eyes burned back at me…the way she caught at her lip, her cheeks still damp and flushed from her nightmare. I wanted to kiss her until she forgot it all. I wanted to kiss her more than I can ever remember wanting to before. The sight of one shoulder exposed, of her nipples, teasing points as they pressed through the thin fabric of her T-shirt…

She was distressed—dazed, even—and I was no better than a horny teenager. Frustrated as hell at myself when I should have been focusing on her wellbeing and her wellbeing alone.

And then she had the audacity to taunt me with the possibility of my bringing another woman home. As if I could even *think* of anyone else with her unique brand of temptation on such flagrant display.

It took every ounce of strength for me to turn and walk away, and she made me do it twice over. Forcing me to turn back each time and drink her in.

The attraction was so fierce off the back of that drive to protect her. Her dream and her distress luring out feelings I've been trying to suppress since the moment she walked into Charles's office.

Did she see how much I wanted her? Did she

see it and panic—throw the idea of other lovers out there with the intention of keeping that line drawn? As a reminder that whatever this is between us, it isn't *that*?

I stride to my bed, tug the quilt back on top, but sleep is impossible.

I reach for my phone and unlock the screen. There she is, in all her Instagram glory. She wasn't kidding when she said she had followers... thousands and thousands of them. Her photos garner so many likes and comments and it's easy to see why. She's a vision of happiness—stunning, carefree, living her best life.

Stripped to the barest of layers on a cliff-edge, her arms outstretched to the blue sky and even bluer waters.

Chilling on a beach with a coconut tipped to her mouth, the juice escaping her lips, trailing down her neck, her chest, beneath her loose-fitting vest...

I move on swiftly.

To a rainforest with colours as vibrant as her, wildlife of various shapes and sizes, all coaxing a smile from her and filling her eyes with joy.

Sunset on a veranda, with a string of light bulbs adding a soft glow, a sofa filled with plush cushions and her, with her head in some guy's lap, his eyes on her face as she grins up at him. A boyfriend, perhaps, a passing friend...

My grip tightens around the phone and I scroll past that picture. Back to the wildlife, to her and some cheerful locals in Malaysia, to the canyons and sea adventures.

Back to her and that guy again.

He only appears once. It should be enough to stop the fierce ache in my chest. The desire to have her head in *my* lap like that, looking up at *me* like that. At ease, happy...

I throw the phone back on the bedside table and lie back, stare at the ceiling.

No, she hasn't been lonely. She's happy. Every one of those photos proves it. Gran didn't know what she was talking about.

And now she's stuck here, in the freezing cold Highlands, with the rain and the responsibility. How long before she needs to be free again? To cut her ties and escape back to that life? The lone wolf ready for her next adventure...

Leaving Glenrobin and I, a distant memory once more...regardless of Gran's last wishes.

Then I think about her lying awake too, on the other side of the door, so close and yet so far away. I think of Ted beside her, just as he was all those years ago. Her one true constant, she'd called him.

I think of the pleading look on her tear-stained face as she asked me to give her a chance, and I think of my diligent team of lawyers, now dissecting Gran's will, and I know what I must do. Even though every instinct screams at me not to be so stupid, so weak...

I fork my hand through my hair with a curse,

tell myself it's only three hundred and sixty-three days to go and then…

And then what?

This estate will always bind us on some level.

But being bound by the tangible estate and the intangible chaos inside are very different things, and so long as she keeps the line drawn, I can toe it. I won't take advantage of this situation, just as I refused to back then.

And I certainly won't make the same mistake of thinking that she cares for me as deeply as I once did her.

No. Toe the line, keep things simple…and stay the hell away from her in night clothes.

I turn to switch off my lamp but there's a sound. Movement beyond the door. I stare at it, see the handle start to shift, and my heart launches into my throat.

What is she…?

No, she can't be…

The door opens and I throw my feet to the floor, sit bolt upright…

'Summer?'

CHAPTER NINE

Summer

I'M MUTE. There are no words for the desire racing through my veins. To see him, his body mostly naked, the muscles in his forearms flexing as he grips the edge of his bed and plants his feet firmly on the floor…

My head is empty of any coherent thought save one: *Please don't reject me.*

'Summer?'

He says my name again and I'm so hooked on hearing him say it. His impossibly deep voice, deeper still. His brown eyes, wide and questioning. His body taut with a tension I know I've put there.

I close the distance between us, every breath I take loud in my ears, my heartbeat too.

'You can tell me to leave, Edward, and I will.' I know I need to tell him this before I go any further. Give him an escape if he needs it.

'Leave?'

His frown is delectable, his confusion written in every line of his brow. And, my God, is it sexy. His eyes too. There's a hint of feeling lost, of curiosity, and then he glances lower and the burn is there. The burn that gives me the confidence to close in.

In my gut, I know he's fighting the same battle as

me. That his tension is about the fear of what comes next. But if you don't think about the future…if you only think about the here and now and the pleasure it can bring…then fear is a waste of energy.

Energy that can be expended in far more satisfying ways.

I rest a hand on his naked shoulder, catch his sharp intake of breath, the jolt that runs through him. He's all hot, hard heat beneath my tingling palm, and the contact is enough to send tiny sparks of electricity coursing through my veins.

'Do you know what you're doing?'

His eyes lift to mine, his voice so raw it rasps over me as powerful as any caress, though his grip on the bed fails to ease. Still fighting. Still resisting.

I slip myself between his legs, raise my palm to his other shoulder. 'Do *you*?'

His Adam's apple bobs…his jaw pulses.

And then I lower my head to his. Slow enough to let him stop me if he so desires…slow enough to let the anticipation build. There's a flush to his cheeks—a flush I feel right through to my core. I search his gaze, the glow of the bedside lamp lancing his darkened depths with gold.

'Edward,' I whisper, our noses almost touching, 'I've wanted this for so long. And I think you want me too. I don't need endearments. I don't need words or empty promises. All I need is you. Tonight.'

And then I kiss him, and it's like I've never kissed a man before. The lightest sweep of my lips over his and the contact pulses through me in a surge of heat so powerful that my knees weaken and my limbs turn molten. But I don't fall because he's got me, his hands flying to my thighs, tugging me against him, and his tongue is delving inside my mouth, his groan so fierce, filled with passion, with surrender.

There's no restraint. No composure. And I revel in it. In the way his hands rake with desperation over my skin, in his tongue as it twists and tangles with my own…

Our breaths are ragged and in tune…our bodies vibrating with such need it feels impossible to get enough. Enough oxygen. Enough sensation. Enough of one another. And I want his all.

'Summer…'

He growls into my mouth, his fingers rough in my hair as I straddle his hips, ride against the ridge of his desire. He tears his mouth away, his groan verging on pained as his erection reaches for me and he holds me back.

'This is a bad idea.'

'Sometimes bad ideas are the most rewarding kind.' I kiss him again, lower my hand between us to caress him, and his thighs shudder beneath me. 'Don't you agree?'

'Yes!' He curses. *'Yes!'* But he tugs my hand

away, his eyes firing up at me. 'I'd like to make it last, though.'

Make it last... If only this kind of pleasure could last for ever...

I block the worrying train of thought and chuckle low in my throat, rake my fingers through his hair, deepen the kiss, think about the now, not what comes next.

His palms come to my aid, slipping beneath my tee. I suck in a breath, arch back as the heat of anticipation floods my breasts. My nipples press against the fabric, hard and desperate... desperate for that first touch. From Edward. My teenage heartthrob. My lifelong dream.

I'm delirious. Intoxicated. My fingers claw into his shoulders as he cups each curve. His touch softens, his caress light and teasing. I bite my lip, look down at him as he rolls each pleading peak with his thumbs. I whimper, writhe, nurse the budding sensation...

'You feel incredible...look incredible...' Awe is in his voice, in his eyes as they burn into his touch. 'Even better than I imagined.'

Has he imagined it? Somewhere deep my heart considers the possibility, but I don't want my heart involved in this.

This is sex. Easy to pigeonhole. Compartmentalise. No deeper meaning. No heart.

But I'm drowning in his gaze, his fevered touch.

Strings are being tugged that I have no control over…

His name is a hoarse cry on my lips as I tear my top from my body and throw it aside, take pleasure from his eyes that burn ever deeper. I feel powerful, empowered… I press him back into the bed and tease my body over him, our underwear the only barrier between us.

'Do you have protection?' I whisper.

He squeezes his eyes shut on a hoarse curse, holds me tight against him.

'You don't?' Disappointment swamps me.

'No, Summer.' His eyes open, pierce mine. 'This wasn't— I never imagined—'

'No, neither of us did.' I nip my lip and say meekly, 'But I'm on the pill.'

His jaw pulses, his grip around my hips too. 'It's not enough.'

My brows draw together. Does he not trust me? Does he think I've been unsafe? Or is he worried about himself?

He moves before I can, sliding my body beneath his as his lips claim mine in a kiss so thorough I wonder if it's goodbye. But then his hands are moving down my front, his mouth too… He's trailing kisses along my jaw, nipping at my earlobe as his fingers trace invisible patterns over my skin, teasing swirls that have me writhing and whimpering.

And then his mouth surrounds one nipple, and I throw my head back with a cry. 'God, yes!'

A quiet voice at the back of my mind, the negative one, wants to ask what he's doing? What does *It's not enough* mean? But I can't form a word past the luscious heat inside me, the heated coil that's being wound tighter and tighter.

His fingers reach the lace of my thong and tease gently, deepening the pressure, circling and circling, until my toes curl into the bed and I can feel the edge so very near.

'Edward, please…please, I need you.'

He slips his hand beneath the fabric. 'I know, baby. I know.'

But his fingers are working their magic, coaxing me higher and higher. *Baby.* He called me baby. He's never…not before… I'm panting as he parts me, his touch gentle, dizzying, hypnotic as he circles directly over me. His thighs trap my own, his fingers slipping inside. His thumb is rolling and rolling… And then his teeth scrape over my nipple and pleasure-pain rips through me.

'Edward!'

'Go with it, baby. Go with it.'

Baby. Baby. The endearment is killing me even as he takes me to the precipice. I claw his shoulders. I toss my head against the pillow, throw it forward to stare down at him. This is real. So *real*.

And I'm gone. My body is pulsing with an orgasm so intense, so mind-blowing, so fierce, that I feel like I've lost something of myself. Lost it and gifted it to him.

I'll never get it back.

And I'm not sure I want to.

Edward

I feel her pleasure like my own. Watching her come apart—so wild, so free, so attuned to me—was breathtaking, and perfect, and more than I ever imagined it could be.

She sags into the bedsheets, her orgasm leaving her limp, and I climb back up her body, kiss a path all the way to her lips.

Could I ever get enough of this? Of her?

Wild laughter punctuates the silence in my brain.

Hell, no. Now I've tasted her I want more. So much more.

And I know this is bad…so very, very bad. I should have sent her back to her room. But I've never wanted anyone like I want her. It would be like Santa gifting you something you've wanted for an entire lifetime and you saying, *Thanks, but no thanks.*

I'm not that stupid.

And you don't think this is more stupid…?

I drown out the inner scorn with an all-consuming kiss, and she gives a blissful murmur deep within her throat.

'You sound sleepy…' I say.

'Do I?'

It's all husky and filled with post-coital warmth.

I stretch out beside her, her back to my front, and hold her to me, nuzzle the skin beneath her ear. 'Yes.'

She gives a soft little laugh, her arms wrapped over mine. 'I'm still on Malaysian time. I don't think I've slept properly for days.'

'Then sleep.'

'But you… I want to…' She draws the words out, all hushed as she snuggles in closer, and the teasing friction of her bum is enough to make my eyes roll.

'Sleep, Summer.'

It's practically a growl in her ear, and she gives the softest murmur of agreement, sleep claiming her whether she wants it to or not.

And I relax against her, savour the warmth of her body, her scent on the air. She feels so right like this. In my arms. She always did. Even as friends there was an ease with which we'd touch, hug, collapse on a bed together…often laughing. I press a kiss to her hair, breathe her in…

That was before she broke you, though.

I squeeze my eyes shut to the pain. Remind myself that this is temporary. Tell myself it's better to have shared something instead of nothing… but not everything.

Because to make love to her fully and let her walk away, as I know she one day will…

I don't think I could come back from that.

CHAPTER TEN

Summer

I WAKE ALONE in Edward's bed. The door between our rooms is still open but it's eerily quiet, not a hint of movement from the bathroom or the dressing room either.

He's gone.

Part of me is surprised he didn't pick me up and put me back in my own bed while I slept.

Another part is surprised that he left without waking me.

Then I see the time and groan. It's almost eleven! *Eleven!*

I curse and throw off the quilt. The cold air of the room assaults my naked body and I shudder… But then I remember why I'm wearing only panties, and just like that I'm on fire again. Recalling his touch, his fingers, his mouth…

Oh, God.

I press a hand to my lips, which thrum with the memory, my smile irrepressible.

What a night! Perfect right up until the point…

I cringe. He took care of me and I repaid him with *sleep.*

And what now? I have no idea where we stand…

Why didn't he wake me? Does he regret it already? Are we going to have to do the morning-after dance?

I fork my fingers through my riotous hair and grip my scalp with a groan. This wasn't how it was supposed to go.

No? How exactly did you picture it going, then?

I don't know. That's the honest answer. I didn't want to know. I just… I just didn't want to wake up without him.

I try to push the disappointment aside and ignore the unease worming its way through my gut.

Get dressed. Go and find him. Deal with it.

The sight of my T-shirt neatly folded on the dressing table eases my shoulders a fraction. He didn't bolt so fast as to leave my clothing on the floor. Maybe that means something.

I return to my bedroom and get ready in record time, opting for a thick green sweater, jeans and the simplest of make-up. I'm keen to get any awkwardness out of the way and reassure him that nothing has changed. Absolutely nothing at all. Not for me at any rate.

I recall the warmth in his brown eyes when he came to me in the night, the concern, the understanding… We may not have the ease and the trust we once had, but we're in a better place than we were in Mr McAllister's office and that has to mean something.

Unless you've ruined it all by seducing him…

I shoot the thought down as I bolt from my

room, racing down the stairs only to find James in the hall, waiting for me. He steps forward as soon as he spies me, his kind smile alleviating the niggle of guilt that I've been caught rising so late.

Not to mention whose bed I rose from.

'Good morning, Summer, I trust you slept well.'

'I did, thank you.' My cheeks burn as I remember the reason for that particular feat and I avoid his eye. 'Have you seen Edward?'

I wince at the pitch to my voice—*way to go in sounding normal.*

'Indeed. Mr Fitzroy breakfasted at seven-thirty and is now in his study working.'

'Seven-thirty?'

Okay, so I probably shouldn't be that surprised, but bearing in mind he was up in the middle of the night seeing to me…

My cheeks flush deeper. Not the best way to phrase it!

'Every weekday,' James says. 'Mr Fitzroy visits the gym at six and expects breakfast to be ready no later than seven-thirty.'

Well, that explains the physique…

'If you'd like to go through to the dining room, I'll send for some food.'

'Oh, no, it's fine, James. I'll sort myself out in the kitchen.'

'But meals are always served in the dining room.'

I almost back down in the face of his frown. I

know I'm messing with his routine, but the idea of eating in the dining room is enough to rob me of my appetite. It was okay with Edward's presence filling the vast space so easily the night before, but eating there alone…

'I'd like to catch up with Marie, anyway.'

'I see…'

I smile the brightest of smiles. 'Thank you, though.'

I'm already heading towards the kitchen and I feel his perplexed gaze follow me. Not that I can blame him. I'm hardly what he's used to. From what I understand, Katherine stopped fostering a decade ago, when she felt she could no longer give the children what they needed. It's likely James wasn't here when kids like me walked the halls.

I have to pass Edward's study to get to the kitchen, and even though I know he's working I figure it wouldn't hurt to peep in…test the water, so to speak.

Before I can lose my nerve, I rap gently on the door, push it open a crack. My eager gaze finds him instantly. He's at his desk, his dark shirt setting off his dark hair and even darker eyes. His phone is to his ear, but his attention in that split-second is all for me. It's as though a trail of gunpowder connects us and the fuse has been lit, with the flame crossing the distance and running right through me.

I breathe through the sensation, smile and wave, mouth *Morning*.

A pulse twitches in his jaw…his lashes flutter. 'Yes, sorry, Juan,' he says into the phone. 'I'm still here.'

And then he dips his head to me, the briefest of nods.

Is that all I'm getting?

His attention shifts to his computer and I have my answer.

I ignore the pang in my chest…the little bubble of panic that threatens.

We're grown adults. We can have sex and be okay. Hell, it wasn't even sex. Just a bit of a fumble. Nothing major.

I'm still telling myself this when I get to the kitchen and the sound of Marie's singing reaches me, coaxing out a smile that quietens the nagging doubt.

'Still singing the same tunes?'

She spins on the spot, palm pressed to her bosom. 'Ah, Miss Summer, you are awake at last!'

Her cheeks round with her smile and I step inside the inviting warmth of the room, breathe in the scent of fresh-baked goodies and am transported back twenty years.

The kitchen hasn't changed at all. The same Belfast sink sits before the window with its view of the garden beyond and a vase of freshly cut flowers on its sill. The same dinner service fills the same antique cabinet along one wall. The same cream range sits beside the fire that always seems to be lit. The same oak table stretches down the middle, the ceiling rack above it laden with pots and pans, herbs and utensils.

'You know, you really can just call me Summer, Marie.'

'Pish-posh. You were Miss Summer back then; you'll be Miss Summer now… That is until you find yourself a good man to take care of you.'

'I don't need a man, Marie. I'm quite capable of taking care of myself.'

'And where's the fun in that?'

There's a twinkle in her eye, and suddenly I feel like all last night's escapades are written in my face for anyone to read.

'I don't know about fun…' I grumble '…it's certainly less trouble.'

'More pish-posh. Now, sit. You need to eat. You're far too skinny!'

'I'm really not.'

But I do exactly as she asks, pulling out a stool at the table and sitting myself down. There's no point insisting I get my own food. Marie wouldn't allow me to do it back then, and she'll be even less inclined to let me do it now.

'Still a coffee fiend?' she asks.

'Still a mother hen?'

She laughs with me as she sets the coffee going. 'It's so good to see you… I can't tell you! Though

I have to say your travels kept both Ms Katherine and I very entertained. Your postcards were the highlight of our month, and we always shared a cuppa over your emails.'

I smile. 'I did try and get Katherine to follow my social media accounts, but I think that was a step too far.'

'Ha! Not through a lack of trying, mind you, but those apps are a minefield. Far safer to get your news from the horse's mouth than be exposed to all that.'

I frown and laugh in one. 'Fair enough.'

'Now!' She claps her hands together. 'What can I get you? How about a fresh roll stuffed with bacon and lashings of tomato sauce?'

My mouth salivates at the very idea. 'You remember my favourite.'

'Of course! I'll get it made while you fill me on your latest travels.'

'And you can get me up to speed on this place.'

And keep me distracted from the epic mistake I might have made...

'Deal.'

Edward

I'm working. Concentrating so hard that my head aches and my eyes sting against the glare of my screen. Not that I can tell you what I've been looking at for the past hour...and it's that realisation that has me shoving away from my desk and scowling up at the portrait of Gran above the fire.

It's not Gran I see, though. It's all Summer.

She's been a permanent presence since I left her side, dragging myself away from her curled up in my bedsheets, all blissful and serene and unwittingly calling me back. And then she appeared in my doorway, temptation personified, and I behaved no better than an arse. All because I was angry with myself for letting her in again.

Juan, my closest friend and my Director of Legal Affairs, called me out on my preoccupation, my need for him to repeat himself several times over rousing his curiosity…

Hell, if the man knew the cause was a woman, he'd be sending for the doctor.

I don't get distracted.

I live for my work.

And a challenge like the failing start-up we'd recently acquired and were trying to discuss was my catnip.

Until Summer's return…

I push up out of my seat and stalk to the window. It's frosty outside, a low mist sweeps across the grounds and the far-off loch, coating everything it touches in a veil of glittering white.

Gran loved it like this…all mystical and full of the fairy tale magic she lived for. The kind of magic that saw her doing this…forcing Summer and I back together. Her will, those letters, her last wishes…

You were the one who let her back in, though. You were the one unable to tune out your heart when nothing good can come of it.

I curse, desperate to reinstate the walls around my heart, the armour that has protected me for years.

But what if Gran was right? What if we're meant to be? What if Summer could change? Be happy here?

My head is shaking before I even finish the thought. I wasn't worth sticking around for before—why would now be any different? My only hope is to keep my distance, and I know how laughable that sounds when we live under the same roof.

Aye, good luck with that, I can almost hear Gran say—before a very real commotion from the entrance hall has me heading that way.

I'm already through the door before I question who or what I might find, and whether I really want to face it. But I *am* questioning it seconds later, when I'm rooted to the spot by the sight of a delighted Summer, all laughter and light, as she hunches over Rufus, Gran's four-legged adoptee and the cause of all the noise.

'Rufus! Rufus!'

Danny, our gamekeeper, bursts in, a rifle under one arm, a dog's lead in the other.

'Get back here!'

The young lad skids to a halt as he spies me, his freckled face even redder than usual, his auburn hair wild beneath his flat cap.

'I'm so sorry, Mr Fitzroy, sir. I was just about to get his lead on when he got wind of your guest and that was it—he was off!'

Summer snaps her head around to see me and straightens just as quickly. 'Edward!'

I tug my gaze from her to Danny. 'It's quite all right, Danny.'

'I imagine he's happy to see you too, sir. He couldn't wait to get back in here. I think he's missed the place; my house is all well and good, but this—this is his home.'

'He *lives* here?' Summer asks, and I know what she's thinking.

In the shock of it all, I haven't even considered Rufus and where he might fit in the future of Glenrobin...the future we're now a part of.

I force myself to hold her eye and try to ignore the way my body worships her. 'Summer, meet Rufus. He's—'

The dog gives an excited bark at the sound of his name and scurries towards me. His paws are high on my chest before I know what he's about, his tongue making a determined sweep for my cheek. I press him down, forgetting what I'd been about to say as his ungodly stench reaches me.

'When did he last have a bath, Danny!'

Through his thick eyebrows, Rufus blinks his doleful eyes at me and whines.

'I know… I'm sorry, sir.' Danny removes his cap and scratches the back of his head. 'But he hates water. I'm surprised he hasn't scarpered at the mere mention of the B-word.'

'Oh, but he's gorgeous!' Summer exclaims, her excited voice calling Rufus back and he's skidding up against her, quick as a flash. His shaggy mass of black, grey and white hair all a blur.

'Aren't you, darling?'

Her laugh lights me up from head to toe. Her eyes so bright as she tickles his eager head, not a care in the world for the smell that's radiating off him.

'And doesn't he know it,' mumbles Danny.

'So, if this is Rufus…' she looks up '…who might you be?'

Well done on introducing the human, Edward…

I want to roll my eyes at myself.

Danny clutches his cap to his chest, stands to attention. 'Danny, the Glenrobin gamekeeper, at your service, ma'am.'

She turns the full wattage of her smile on him now, and I feel the most ridiculous surge of jealousy. That he's earned it where as I clearly haven't.

And can you blame her after your cold greeting earlier?

'It's a pleasure to meet you, Danny. I'm Summer.'

She offers her hand and he gives it a hearty shake, his redness reaching new heights.

'And you, Miss Summer.' He gestures to Rufus, who is now nuzzling the inside of Summer's palm. 'He certainly likes you.'

She smiles down at the smelly mass of fur. 'And I like him.'

'He's been mighty moody since Ms Katherine passed away…it's good to see a spring in his step again.'

'So he was Katherine's dog?'

Danny nods. 'She found him on the grounds here when he was a pup—quite wild by all accounts. We reckon he's a cross between an Irish Wolfhound and a Bearded Collie.'

'He's not a working dog, then?' Her gaze goes to the doorway, where Danny's three black Labrador Retrievers wait patiently for their master, probably despairing of their little runaway friend.

'Och, no. He's all about the fun, this one.'

Fun. Summer's middle name.

'In that case,' she chirrups, 'I think we're going to get along famously.'

'Are you ready to have him back, then, sir?' Danny looks to me.

'Back?' And now I sound like the dim-witted fool I am. 'Of course. Yes.'

'Does this mean he's now *ours*?' she asks me tentatively, and I get it…feel the whole 'ours' thing making me squirm and warm in one.

I scratch the back of my head, the move reminding me of Danny doing exactly the same thing. What is it about Summer that has a man's temperature rising, the collar of his shirt tightening and his hormones regressing to uncontrollable teenage levels again?

'I guess you could say he belongs to the castle,' I correct, as if that somehow sounds better. 'When Gran couldn't take in foster children any more and Rufus appeared—well, you can just imagine her joy.'

Her smile widens, her happiness so pure as her eyes fall to Rufus, who is now leaning into her, his head huge against her waist.

I screw my face up as a cold gust blows through the open door, sweeping his wet dog scent right into my face. 'But a bath first, Danny, and then he can come home.'

Rufus whines, his ears pricking at the dreaded word, and Summer pipes up, 'I'll do it.'

Both Danny and I gape at her.

'He really does hate water, miss,' says Danny.

She gives a shrug. 'It's okay. I've had my fair share of working with tricky animals—and humans—over the years. Does the boot room still have a shower?'

'Yes…' I say, my frown deep. She can't be serious…

'Ms Katherine used to hose him down in there,' Danny says, all helpful. 'His stuff should still be in there—shampoo, towels, brushes… But if you need anything, you just let me know.'

'Great. You can trust me with him, Danny. I promise.'

She's already back to fussing over Rufus, and Danny is grinning like a fool, his eyes as joyful as the dog at her feet as he watches them both.

I clear my throat. 'Danny?'

The man starts, his eyes shooting to me as his body straightens and he seems to give himself a mental slap. 'Yes, sir?'

'Is everything okay with the estate? I wanted to talk to you about the food reserves with the freak weather that's been forecast…'

He nods rapidly, all business now. 'I wanted to talk to you about the same. If it's anything like the snow a couple of years back we'll be needing to supplement it for a good while.'

'I'd say a few months at least, while the ground thaws out. Let's take a walk and discuss it.' *And get out of Summer's distracting orbit.* 'I'll get my coat.'

I'm already heading to the rear of the house when Summer races up behind me, accompanied by the scurry of Rufus's claws on the wooden floor.

'I'll get mine too.'

'You're not needed for this, Summer.'

'But I want to come. If I'm to—if we're to live here—I should get to know the lay of the land.'

I shake my head, give a soft huff.

'What?' she asks.

I say nothing as I shove open the door to the boot room and grab a weatherproof coat from the hook.

'What, Edward? Are you implying that because I'm a woman I can't—?'

'No, Summer!' I spin to face her and she's wide-eyed. Even Rufus has frozen. 'It has nothing to do with you being a woman and everything to do with you. Who you *are*.'

'What—? What are you saying?'

I shake my head, choke on a laugh that feels more like a sob. 'Playing at house. Acting serious, like you're going to stick around this time. When just last night you reiterated how you never stay in one place long enough to settle, to create a home.'

'But… Edward, this is different. I want to do what Katherine requested. I want to play my part and look after this place.'

'How long for, Summer? A month? Two…?'

How could she not see how much this was killing me? Or maybe she could and she simply didn't care?

'You know how long for.'

'Oh, that's right—a year. And then you'll leave and not look back.'

'No. It won't be like that.'

I stare down at her hard, trying desperately to calm my pulse. My anger stems from my panic, not her. This isn't her fault. She doesn't deserve my wrath. Gran has put us in this situation and I only have myself to blame for wanting more…so much more than Summer will ever want to give.

I force my shoulders to ease, my voice to soften. 'Whatever the case, you don't need to be involved in this. I've been running the estate for Gran long enough. I know the staff, the routine, the responsibility.'

She wets her lips. 'But I don't want to be a spare part. I like to keep busy.'

And don't I know it? Always dashing from one thing to the next, one country to the next even, probably fearful that her feet might get stuck.

'You're not a spare part. Like you said last night, you have the time and the freedom to carry on Gran's good work. So do it, Summer. Go and do some good and I'll take care of managing the estate.'

I shove my arms into the jacket, make for the door.

'But Edward, I thought—last night—that we—'

She breaks off, her eyes searching mine, as if I can somehow finish that sentence for her. But my mind is racing, remembering her in my arms, her coming apart around my touch, calling out my name, that earth-shattering connection…

Breathe. Speak.

'Last night— Last night was a mistake. We were both in a weird head-space. Returning here, the inheritance, the memories, your nightmare… all of it.'

'You want to pretend it didn't happen?' she asks quietly. 'That it didn't…didn't mean something?'

'Yes, Summer, that's exactly what I want.'

'But we're okay, right?'

I take a stilted breath. 'We're fine,' I lie. 'Have a good day, Summer.'

I don't wait for her to respond. I up my pace and join Danny on the front porch, throwing my focus into him and off the woman with the haunted blue gaze who had looked close to tears as I left.

Was it cruel, after what we'd shared the night before, to dismiss it so readily to her face?

But what was the alternative? To acknowledge it? To admit that it had meant something? To admit that I want more—so much more?

'Dammit all!'

'Sorry, sir?'

Danny's frowning up at me.

'Nothing. Sorry. Let's go.'

Before I race back inside and beg for forgiveness…and for the future I know we can't have.

Summer

'Don't you worry about him, Rufus.' I tickle his head, though I'm talking more to myself as I watch Edward's swiftly departing form. 'He's only in a grump because he doesn't know how to handle last night. He'll come round.'

I hope.

'And in the meantime, it's bath time, buddy.'

He gives the same whimper and I smile at him, hunch down to his level.

'It'll be fun, I promise.'

'Fun' becomes a very interesting and very wet game of hide-and-seek, with Rufus trying to hide his huge frame and me trying to wash him and not the entire boot room. But we get there eventually, and if I say so myself he smells divine.

'One job down, buddy. Plenty more to go!'

Like carrying on Katherine's legacy…

It would've been good to talk through some ideas with Edward—though I have a feeling he'd caution me to walk before I can run. But I'm excited. I've never had the means to do good on such a level.

I've volunteered in exchange for bed and board in places across the globe—Asia, Africa, Latin America—and I've repaired homes, built classrooms, clinics, taught English, given love and care to kids who need it. But to have money now… enough money to give back on an entirely different scale… The idea fills me with enthusiasm and an impatience to act.

And heaven knows I need the distraction, with Edward's tormented gaze and parting words plaguing me, threatening to replay over and over until I want to run away and not look back. Proving I'm no better than I was all those years ago.

But I *am* better. I *am* stronger. I know my own worth and I'm determined to do right by Katherine if it's the last thing I do.

As for Edward's reaction… I can't blame him for being wary, for keeping me at a distance—not with our history and with the way I live my life now. Doesn't make his dismissal any easier to bear, though…

I head upstairs, with Rufus on my tail, and change out of my wet clothes into something comfy and warm.

Now what?

I look at Rufus at my feet. 'How about a tour?' He gives his approval in the form of a bark. 'Getting my bearings again counts as walking before running, right?'

We set off together, and his company goes some way towards softening Edward's chilling departure. I give silent thanks to Katherine for another unexpected gift, while the real gift, the estate itself, brings back so many memories.

The castle is much the same—aside from the bathrooms, which have been upgraded, the surprising lift that's been added at the heart of the castle, and the cinema room that's like a miniature theatre. But as we approach my old bedroom I can see the degradation, the damp that needs treating, the floors that need stripping, the walls that need re-papering.

I reach my bedroom door, see the heart made from wicker still hanging there and brush my fingers over it, a bittersweet smile on my lips.

Rufus nudges my hand and I look down at him. 'This was my room, buddy, once upon a time.'

I twist the knob and push the door open. The hinges protest as if they haven't been used in years, and inside the daylight is dimmed by the thin drapes that are drawn across the window. Dust sheets cover the furniture, the bunk beds are stripped, and the walls… The walls are still covered in the same pink and white wallpaper, depicting flamingos and clouds.

For a moment I just stand there, taking it all in. Edward's right—it needs work. The damp is worse here, building around the windows, in the corners, and there's a certain chill in the air… But none of it detracts from the memories. I can still hear the laughter in the walls. Still imagine the kids running around and me trying to mind my own business, my head in a travel book, dreaming of the adventures I would one day experience.

'And I got to go on those adventures,' I say, looking down at Rufus, who cocks his head at me. 'Lucky me, hey?'

But as I stand in the room I once planned my future in I can't shift the feeling that something went wrong. Because the sense of achievement,

of fulfilment, never came. All those adventures…
all those things on my bucket list…and not once
did I feel at peace. Happy. Content.

Katherine's letter haunts me…her warning
too…

*I worry that if you're not careful life will
pass you by and you will never pause long
enough to feel what it is to be content, to be
happy, to be loved…*

But maybe I'm broken. Maybe fulfilment is
something that will always feel out of reach for
me. Or maybe I just haven't experienced enough
yet.

*Or maybe Katherine is right. Because you felt
pretty content when you were in Edward's arms
last night, didn't you?*

I gulp the thought down. I won't accept it. I
don't need another human being to feel happy
and fulfilled. The only person who can give me
that is myself.

'Isn't that right, Rufus?'

A bark. Definite agreement.

And getting started on Katherine's legacy is
sure to be a step in the right direction.

'Come on, buddy. I have charities to speak to,
fundraising events to organise, and I know just
where to start…'

I stride back to my new bedroom and take up

the photograph of me and Katherine, the two of us surrounded by preparations for the Halloween Fairy Tale Ball.

The thirty-first of October is a month away… It's possible to pull off a ball in that time, surely?

'Anything's possible if you set your mind to it, Summer.'

Katherine's soft voice wraps around me, encourages me.

'What do you reckon, Rufus? I've got this, right?'

His bark is more of a whine-cum-groan, and his eyes peeping through his heavy eyebrows are far too sceptical, reminding me of Edward and his cautionary tone…

'It's an idea. Though it's a lot of work…organising such affairs, I mean.'

And if ever I needed added motivation, that was it, right there.

CHAPTER ELEVEN

Summer

GLENROBIN IS IN CHAOS. Literally.

There are boxes everywhere and James is my eager assistant. If someone had told me two weeks ago that James, the estate's very austere butler, is a secret dance lover with a penchant for fairy tales, I would have rolled over laughing. But it's true.

Today we're taking delivery of the background pieces that will set the scene of the ball, and Rufus is as giddy as we are, thinking it's an assault course for his pleasure alone.

'Right, I think if we get these shifted into the ballroom as soon as—'

'What the blazes?'

Edward tumbles into the hall, his feet caught on one of the many boxes, and both James and I cringe, unable to save him. He rights himself quickly enough, with a bounding Rufus more of a hindrance than a help, but the giant dog is unperturbed by Edward's death stare.

'I'm sorry, sir. I'll have this cleared right away.'

'It's my fault,' I'm quick to say over James. 'I insisted we check the items off on the inventory before moving the boxes.'

The death stare is upon me, and for the briefest

second I see the flare of something in his eyes before the look is replaced with the one I have come to expect these past two weeks. A look that would turn the warmest heart to stone.

'What is all this?'

'It's for the ball,' I say with forced calm. 'You know…the Halloween ball I *told* you I was arranging.'

His eyes return to the boxes, widening with what I'd like to think *isn't* alarm. Has he not listened to me at all?

I've had my suspicions, but seriously…

Never mind being told that James is a dance fiend—if someone had told me it was possible to live with someone and tune them out so completely, I'd have told them they were talking nonsense. But Edward has proved otherwise, and I don't want to acknowledge how much it hurts… or how much the staff have picked up on it too.

I've barely seen him since our night together. When he's at home he's confined to his study, working. On the rare occasions he emerges his phone is in hand, his eyes fixed on it. At breakfast, his tablet is his companion. Lunch he takes in his study. Dinner is the only time he graces me with his presence, and even then his mind is elsewhere and we dine in virtual silence.

Not that I've pined for him. Not in the slightest. Honest.

I've spent my time reacquainting myself with

the castle and the grounds, trying hard to feel comfortable…at home. I'm so glad of Rufus, who has become my little shadow—okay, my *big* shadow. And of James and Marie, who've been so warm and welcoming, trying hard to make up for Edward's noticeable aloofness.

And I'm so excited to be putting Katherine's money to good use, and her name too, by holding the Halloween ball in her honour.

I've spoken to the local children's home, social services too. They're as keen as me. Katherine's name gets me prompt access to anyone I need, and it's amazing how time isn't an issue when you offer to pay a premium at the last minute. I have charities, caterers, entertainers, set designers, the all-important attendees with big wallets, and guests—young and old—all lined up.

It's going to be the party of the year and I can't wait!

The only thing that takes the edge off the thrill is Edward. I've been desperate to discuss my ideas, to engage him, get his sign-off on the plans—the lot. He'd know about it all inside out if he chose to listen.

Instead he's snubbed every conversation I've attempted, and there's only so much snubbing one girl can take.

Which is why his blank look now makes my blood boil.

I want to stomp right over to him and dare him

to take issue with me. A fight would beat the silence I've been treated to this past fortnight. But there's a small part of me—the part that still feels guilty about leaving all those years ago—that holds me back.

'And when is it?'

I gape at him, fold my arms across my chest, tap my foot. 'It's a *Halloween* ball, Edward, when do you think it is?'

He rakes a hand through his hair, blows out a breath. It's then that I notice the lines around his eyes, the shadows beneath too… Did I do that to him?

'Right…right, of course.'

'Look…' I soften both my posture and my tone '…we'll have it cleared away very soon.'

He doesn't look reassured, and if James wasn't a captive audience I'd press him on what the issue is—the real issue. Because it's not the boxes. And if we don't have it out soon, those shadows under his eyes are only going to get worse—as is the atmosphere within the castle walls.

'Just tell me you have a handle on the budget for this event. It does need to *raise* money, not lose it.'

And just like that I'm livid again. I've been working hard around the clock, and James has too, and he has the nerve to question—

The antique doorbell rings through the hall, silencing my inner rant as all eyes look to the entrance.

'That'll be Juan.'

Edward's already moving off, hopping over the boxes to get to the door, unaware that he's leaving me steaming.

'We'll take coffee in my study, James.'

'Of course, sir. As soon as I've got these—'

'*Now*, James!'

Why, the stubborn, obstinate—

'Of course, sir.'

James hurries to put down the box he's holding and I bite my tongue. I want to tell him to forget Edward's rude request, but I don't want to get him into any more trouble.

'I won't be a moment, Summer.'

I give him an understanding smile and off he hurries. My eyes snap to Edward, who's pulling open the door, oblivious to the escalating heat behind him.

'Juan, it's so good to see you!'

His cheeriness is like lighter fuel to my already burning ire and I screw my face up, silently mimic him. *Juan, it's so good to...*

Oh, crap!

Juan is looking past Edward, straight at me, and judging by the sparkle in his eye he saw every second of my performance.

I smile stiffly, eyes wide.

Edward catches his friend's gaze, and if I'm not mistaken the slightest flush reaches into his cheeks. Is he embarrassed by me?

'Juan, meet Summer. Summer, meet Juan—my good friend and colleague.'

'I know who she is. We've already spoken.'

Juan strides towards me, leaving Edward at the door. Rich brown skin, carefully groomed black hair, eyes as friendly and warm as his smile. He is a sight for sore eyes—particularly as I glimpse Edward behind him, with an expression close to thunder.

'It's a pleasure to meet you in person, Summer.'

'And you.' I smile up at him and he leans in, air-kissing both my cheeks in a waft of very expensive aftershave. 'I think Edward's been hiding you away on purpose.'

He throws a teasing look back at his friend and I giggle like a teenager. The light relief is so much better than the anger. Don't get me wrong, I'm still angry, but I'll deal with Edward later.

'Here, I have something for you…'

I sense Edward's curiosity mounting along with the gathering storm as Juan pulls a slip of card from his inside jacket pocket and passes it to me.

'I know you said we could email our RSVP, but I figured since I was heading this way…'

'RSVP?' Edward comes up behind him, frowning down at the pearlescent rectangle with its silver scrawl and embossed fairy tale scene.

'Thank you,' I say.

'You're very welcome.'

'RSVP?' Edward repeats, stronger this time, his brows raised to us both.

'For the Halloween Ball…' I smile sweetly. 'You know…the thing we were just talking about…'

He makes a sound deep within his throat…

Did he just growl at me? Oh, this gets better and better.

'Aww, don't look so put out…' I touch his chest, well aware I'm poking the bear. 'You're invited, too. You're my Prince Charming.'

Juan chokes on a laugh, and I swear I hear Edward curse under his breath. Serves him right. If he'd paid attention, none of this would be a surprise.

I got a grunt from him when I asked for sign-off on the people I intended to invite, another when I said I was going to ask his personal assistant for help, so as far as I'm concerned at this juncture anything goes.

Though I may have made something of a poor judgement call when it came to using Katherine's old guest list as a starting point. I'm either a sucker for punishment or just a tad too soft. In either case it's done now, and the responses are flooding in.

I haven't received *theirs* yet, but never say never…

Perhaps they'll do me an unconscious favour and not attend.

But if they do the black look on Edward's face now might not be the worst I witness in connection with the ball.

'Well, if the weather keeps up,' Juan is saying,

'you'll certainly have the magic of a winter won-
derland to add to your fairy tale theme. I was worried we weren't going to make it.'

I look outdoors, to the blanket of white quickly
thickening, and grimace. 'It'll certainly help keep
the ice sculptures cold, but if the guests can't get
here we won't have a ball at all.'

'Don't you worry yourself with that. Edward
will make sure the roads are clear—won't you,
Edward?'

He slaps his friend on the back...his friend who
looks as if he might want to string someone up
right now... And I'm not sure if it's me or Juan,
my new and wonderful comrade-in-arms.

'Excellent. So I can leave that job in your capable hands—yes, my Prince?'

I bat my eyelashes at him and suppress a laugh
at the look on his face. Okay, so maybe 'my
Prince' was a step too far, but winding him up is
so much fun. Payback of a sort.

'I'll take care of it.'

It's a grumble under his breath, and for the added
fun of it I leap up at him, kiss his cheek. His warmth
teases at my lips, his scent at my nose, and all that
strength beneath my palm flexes as I lean into him.

Oh, heaven.

'Thank you.'

His eyes collide with mine, their depths wild and
dangerous, and then I'm dropping back and turning away before Juan sees more than he should.

I feel the thrum beneath my skin long after he's gone. And if I had the sense to dwell on it I'd likely be worried. But I don't dwell. I act.

And right now I have boxes to shift and a snow-loving dog to walk.

'Right, Rufus. Boxes and then walk. Deal?'

He gives an animated bark.

'At least you still love me...'

Not the wisest choice of words, Summer...

'It's a figure of speech,' I say into the ether.

Just a figure of speech.

Edward

'You look like you could do with something stronger than coffee.'

I flick Juan a look, wanting to flick him something else, but knowing it's not his fault I'm in this state. I can't sleep. I can't eat. She dominates my every waking and sleeping thought.

I've even found her old postcards to Gran and have been re-reading them all...staying connected to her in a way that feels safe, controlled... And I know how ridiculous that is when she's in the same building as me, but I can't look at her without wanting to do so much more.

He places his cup down and eyes my clenched fist upon the desk. 'Okay, I'm making an executive decision. Coffee isn't going to cut it.'

I force my hand to relax. 'It's only three in the afternoon, Juan.'

'What's the saying? It's party time somewhere… I'll pour, shall I?'

He's already on his feet, striding to the antique Japanese drinks cabinet—Gran's pride and joy.

'I'll say one thing for Katherine: she always had this thing fully stocked. You know, I tried to get my hands on this fifty-year-old malt…' He raises up a bottle '…happy to pay a fair sum for it too, and there was none to be had.'

'She was a woman of many talents.'

'You don't *sound* impressed.'

Impressed? It's Gran's fault I'm in this mess.

'Help yourself to it,' I grind out, pushing up out of my seat and heading to the window.

Summer's laughter reaches me through the glass a second before she appears, a bright splash of colour. Her red coat—another excellent purchase—is flaring out as she spins on the spot, blonde waves escaping her green beanie, an excited Rufus prancing around her, chasing the toy she has in her hand.

She's a vision.

And I should have looked away the moment I heard her.

'I don't mind if I do, so long as you're joining me.'

I drag my eyes from the window to see Juan studying me intently.

'I take it you have your driver here?'

'I do.'

As he says it, the arrival of someone else outside snags my attention. 'So you do…'

Juan's driver approaches Summer, who pauses to offer him a smile, her cheeks all rosy, face aglow. He's young and handsome and his instant attraction towards her is as obvious as Juan's had been.

I force my jaw to relax before I crack a tooth.

She's laughing at something the man has said and I feel an ache deep within my chest, a longing… I want to make her laugh like that again. I want her eyes to sparkle up at me. I want… I want…

The driver is digging in his pocket for something that has Rufus bobbing up and down.

'Does your driver always have dog treats in his pocket?'

Juan chuckles. 'There's a story there.'

'I bet…'

'But I'm more interested in yours right now.'

His tone turns sombre and I refuse to look at him.

'Mine?'

'You haven't been yourself since you came back here.'

I haven't been myself since Summer walked back into my life.

He joins me at the window, a glass in each hand. He passes me one as his eyes drift to the view…to his driver, Rufus, Summer…

'Of course. I understand now.'

'I doubt that.' I sip the warming liquid and wish it would quash the churn beneath my ribs.

'I've never seen you like this. Not over work and certainly not over a woman.'

'I'd love to see how you'd fare being forced into living with one for a year.'

'I told you I would pull the will apart and get you out of it, but you were the one who put a stop to that.'

'Because I can't do it. Gran wanted her to live here—she wanted to give her a home.'

'She wanted you to have a home too.'

I grunt—a really unbecoming habit I seem to have developed.

'You forget I've read the letter—the will too. She was pretty clear about what she wanted and why she chose Summer too…'

'Summer was different. She was special…'

'Special to who? Your grandmother, or…?'

The smallest of smiles touches my lips, and my eyes are lost in the sight of her as I fail to answer him.

'Hey, don't get me wrong—I can totally see the appeal.'

A growl tries to rise up within me. It's a misplaced jealousy that I can't suppress. 'She's off-limits, Juan.'

He lifts his glass to me. 'Amen to that. I wouldn't dare.'

I give a choked laugh, throw back more whisky,

nursing the burn. 'You forget I know you and your whole bed 'em and leave 'em reputation.'

'What's the alternative? End up like you?'

'What's that supposed to mean?'

'Like you need to ask… But, for the record, I'm insulted you think I'd go after someone else's woman.'

'She's not my woman.'

'No?' His brows arch, his grin disbelieving. 'You could have fooled me.'

I say nothing, my eyes still trained on the outdoors, my thoughts far too occupied with her.

'So, if she's not your woman, and if she's nothing to you, what's the real problem here? Because it's clearly not the inheritance that you once saw her as undeserving.'

I force my eyes to meet his and his own eyes narrow. He cocks his head to one side. 'You're in love with her, aren't you?'

'She's been back in my life a fortnight.'

'That's not what I asked.'

I stare at him, mute, my chest tight, my heart twisting, my pulse racing. Do I? Is that why this is killing me? Why the pressure of being around her again, knowing she will eventually leave, is dominating my every thought and I have no control over it?

There's no teasing in Juan's face now. His smile is soft, his eyes sickeningly sympathetic.

'I know I'm not the best advocate for love, but

my aunt swears she knew within seconds of meeting my uncle that he was the one for her. Love at first sight, she reckons—and, hell, they've been married forty years and counting. They're still like those lovesick teenagers who fled Colombia together. It's stomach-turning…but also kind of sweet.'

I give a gruff laugh. 'If I didn't know any better, I'd say you were a little envious.'

'Because you look so good on it yourself?'

He's got you there.

'Look, Edward, if she's the one…and, let's face it, you've walked the earth and bedded enough women to know the difference by now…do something about it.'

'I can't.'

'"Can't" isn't in your vocabulary. You told me that over a decade ago, when I told you we couldn't save that renewable energy company. But we did it. And achieved a whole lot more with it too.'

'That's business.'

'You say potato…' He shrugs. 'Sounds to me like you're just running scared.'

'And what if I am?' I say, sick of fighting it, denying it.

The look of surprise on his face is a picture. 'You really do have it bad.'

I do.

I swallow. Not that I can say it out loud. Not when I have no idea what to do about it.

'So what's the problem? She doesn't like you? Is that it?'

Like me? Ha! She liked me well enough two weeks ago.

Until I shut down and pushed her out.

'She likes me well enough…when I'm not behaving like an arse.'

'So fix the attitude and go after her—what have you got to lose?'

'Her.' That's the simple and painful answer. 'She won't stick around. By her own admission she never stays in one place long enough to form connections, have a relationship…'

'Sounds like someone else I know.'

Another grunt.

'Seriously, look at yourself and your own history—who's to say it won't be different for you both this time?'

I give a huff…but isn't he talking some sense?

'Rather than being an arse, why not try being a man worth sticking around for?'

A flicker of light sparks inside me. Hope. 'Using my own words against me?' I ask.

'Something like that.' He grips my shoulder in encouragement, support. 'You've never been one to shy away from risk in business. So why start now with your personal life?'

CHAPTER TWELVE

Summer

'EDWARD!' MY HEART leaps into my throat as I spy him not two metres away, rooted in the snow as if he's been there a while.

The collar of his coat is drawn high, his hands are deep inside his pockets, and his eyes strike out beneath the rim of a navy beanie. He looks good in a beanie—less executive, more everyday, and my betraying heart gives a little flip as it settles.

How did I miss his approach?

You're rolling around in the snow with a great big Heffalump of a dog and you ask how?

Said Heffalump yaps excitedly as he launches himself at our new arrival. He has none of the wariness I have. But then, Rufus hasn't been shut out like I have.

'Sorry.' Edward reaches down to pat Rufus, but his eyes stay fixed on me. 'I didn't mean to startle you.'

'You didn't. We were just having fun. Has Juan gone?'

Rufus rolls around in front of him, demanding his attention, and Edward rubs his belly, the sight making my skin prickle and my chest bloom with envy.

'Aye.'

I dust snow off my clothing as I step towards him, my anger from earlier weak in the face of this new Edward. Appeasing Edward.

'I'm sorry about the mess in the hall, I just didn't want anything moved until I'd gone through the list.'

'I know. I get it.'

He looks up at me and those soft brown eyes render me speechless, their sudden warmth so unexpected.

'I'm sorry I was such a grump.'

I fold my arms, purse my lips as I side-eye him. 'Have you had another lobotomy?'

He laughs, and the sound is so deep and unrestrained and everything I've been craving since our meeting with Mr McAllister.

'No.' He smiles at me, hesitant now. 'I don't know…maybe.'

And Edward hesitant is as sexy as Edward stripped to his underwear. What's going on?

'Can I join you for a bit?'

My laugh is soft with disbelief. 'You're asking if you can come and play with us?'

'I guess I am.'

'Are you sure you can afford to spend the time away from your desk? Because this past fortnight you've barely looked up from your work.'

He grimaces. 'I know. I'm sorry about that too.'

'You're very apologetic all of a sudden. What did Juan do to you?'

'Talked some sense into me. Just don't tell him I said that.'

He's teasing, but I'm not laughing any more. I'm confused. And I'm hurt. Having him come out here, expecting me to welcome him back like everything is fine. Swinging from hatred to aloof, from moody to this… I can't protect my heart if he keeps taking me by surprise like this.

'Come on, Rufus. I owe you an actual walk.'

I turn away and Rufus scrambles up, trots to my heel as I head towards the woods. I refuse to be a doormat. There's only so far my guilt and past behaviour will excuse his behaviour now.

'Summer!'

I hear his feet crunch swiftly through the snow, feel his presence at my back, but don't turn. 'What?'

'I really am sorry.'

'I heard you.'

'I shouldn't have snapped at you.'

'No, you shouldn't have.'

'I'm sorry for snapping at James too.'

'Good.' I pause to pick up a stick poking out of the snow and throw it for Rufus, who bounds after it. 'Anything else you care to apologise for while you're at it?'

He blows out a breath and Rufus sprints up to

me, drops the stick. But I'm too attuned to Edward behind me, waiting for his answer.

Rufus is jumping up and down, barking with impatience. *This is important, buddy*, I tell him mentally. *It's time for the big bad wolf to play nice.*

'I'm sorry for shutting you out these past two weeks.'

A small smile touches my lips. 'And...?'

I can sense his frown as he racks his brain for more. 'For keeping you out of the estate business and not helping with the preparations for the Halloween ball.'

I take up the stick, give it a good throw. 'I'm glad you finally—'

'And I'm also sorry for this...'

'Huh—?' I start to turn, but too late. He has the collar of my coat in one hand and a ball of snow in the other and...

'Edward!' I gasp as the ice-cold snow breaks through my clothing, and arch against the icy trickle as it runs down my back. 'Why, you...!'

He jumps back. 'Hey, all's fair in love and war.'

I have no idea if he knows what he's saying, but now isn't the time to think about it—not when there's a fight to be had...a physical one full of play.

I'm already bending forward. 'You're going to regret that.'

'Is that a threat?'

'It's a promise.' He's jogging backwards and

I'm balling up snow. 'Have you forgotten how good my aim is?'

He laughs, his eyes so alive, his cheeks so pink. And I'm high on it—high on him.

I take aim and fire, catching his shoulder as he ducks and scoops up his own ball. I turn and run with a squeal, Rufus leaping alongside me. I feel it rather than see it, the dusting to my right as the snowball misses me and disturbs the hedge. Another one comes, quick-fire, and this time Rufus leaps for it, his great big body rolling into me as he catches it. And then we're both tumbling to the ground, the soft snow breaking our fall.

'Summer!'

I can hear Edward's panic, hear his feet pounding through the snow, and I bide my time. Rufus licks my face with a whimper, but I'm concentrating on keeping my eyes closed and my hands full of snow.

Wait. Just wait.

Cold air sweeps over me as he drops to his knees. His breath is hot on my cheek as he leans in, his hands soft on my body.

'Summer! Summer! Are you okay?'

Now!

My eyes snap open, my snow-filled hands come together either side of his face, my grin is triumphant. 'Gotcha!'

'You minx!'

I laugh, wild and free, and he shakes the snow

off, showering me with it, his eyes returning to mine, blazing and full of teasing. But then he stills. The world stills. Our breaths come in short, heavy pants. Puffs of steam fill the narrow gap between us. He's so close. Only inches away.

I swallow, unable to fill my lungs, and even Rufus scoots back onto his haunches with an intrigued whine.

'Summer…?'

It's a groan, a growl, a plea, and then his hands are in my hair, displacing my beanie as he kisses me. And, heaven help me, I'm drowning. Drowning in a sea of sensation. So much cold beneath me, so much heat above, and my hands are in his hair, tugging him closer, anchoring my body higher, pressing against him.

I'm scared that he'll suddenly evaporate…stop kissing me…that this isn't real…it's a daydream… a very real-feeling daydream.

And what about when he wakes up and regrets it? Shuts you out again?

I shove against his chest, break the kiss. 'I can't do this. Not again. You shutting me out—it hurts too much.'

'I'm so sorry, Summer. I never wanted to hurt you.' He cups my face, sweeps his gloved thumbs across my cheeks, his eyes mesmerising in their intensity, their sincerity. 'I just didn't know how to behave…how to move forward…'

'Do you ever think you overthink everything?'

He laughs deep in his throat and it resonates through me, warming and thrilling in one.

'Do you ever think you don't think enough?'

'Hey!' I try to shove myself out of his grasp, but he has me held fast. 'You want more snow flying at you? Because I'm ready to go round two.'

'There's only one kind of round two I'm interested in, and it has nothing to with the bed of snow beneath us and everything to do with the warm variety indoors.'

My breath hitches. 'Are you serious?'

'I've never been more so.'

Panic, excitement, want… It all flutters up, choking at my throat. Can I trust him? I trusted him not to run two weeks ago and look what happened.

'I mean it, Summer. I've been an arse of the highest order. I don't know how long I'll have you back in my life—a week, a month, a year—but I've been so focused on you leaving, on this ending, that I've lost sight of what we can have right now.'

A smile builds with the relief inside me. 'What kind of idiot focuses on the end without enjoying the story first, Edward?'

His eyes glitter…his chuckle deepens. 'What kind, indeed?'

And then he's kissing me, and I'm kissing him, and our bodies are rising up, moving as one.

'Although I think we owe someone a walk,'

I murmur against his lips, and Rufus barks his approval.

Edward presses his forehead to mine, slips his hands around mine. 'Okay. Walk and then...?'

'Walk and then...' I give him a flirtatious wink in confirmation and tug him towards the trail. 'I can fill you in on the plans for the ball while we walk, if you're finally ready to listen, that is...?'

He squeezes my fingers. 'I'm all ears.'

'Well, for starters I'll have you know I have the budget in control.'

He grimaces. 'I know. I trust you. I shouldn't have said that.'

'No, you shouldn't have.' And then I let my excitement for the event take over... 'I'm so excited about it, Edward. I've been using Katherine's old plans as a basis; I want it to pay true homage to her and all that she did. The ice sculptures are an added feature, but the weather is so perfect—and can you imagine the faces of the children as they come up the drive to see horses leaping, princesses dancing, glittering in the moonlight? And the fairy lights I have planned... It's going to be so magical and...'

He's looking at me strangely and my cheeks start to burn. 'What?'

'You know, you're so sexy when you get like this.'

'Like what?'

'Inspired. Passionate.'

I grin. 'I'll remind you of that on the day.'

'What day?'

'The day of the ball…' I wrap my arms around his neck, look up at him, my grin turning impish. 'When you see your costume.'

'My *what*?'

'Did you think Prince Charming was just a name I'd plucked out of thin air?'

'Summer…' He draws out my name, his brows reaching inside his beanie, and I nip my lip again, bite back a giggle.

'It *is* a fairy tale ball, Edward. Costumes are compulsory—especially for you and me as the hosts.'

He frowns. 'Right…silly me.' And then his eyes spark. 'Hang on—if I'm Prince Charming, what does that make you?'

'Cinderella, of course. Quite fitting, don't you think?'

His smile is slow and sultry as he wraps his arms around me, holds me closer. 'Are you saying you're a poor mistreated maiden in need of rescuing?'

'Hardly!' I choke on a laugh. 'I've *never* needed a man to rescue me. However…' I flirt with the hair at the nape of his neck '…I will play the role on the day, if you promise to play yours?'

'Clever, Summer, very clever.'

'Persuasive, I think you mean.'

'Clever, persuasive, cunning…' he drags his

mouth over mine '...and very...' he nips my bottom lip with his teeth '...sexy.'

Edward

We race to the bedroom faster than is deemed normal for fully grown adults who should be able to resist long enough to pass the household staff without arousing suspicion, but it's like we're possessed. The frenzied heat coursing through our veins pushing out all sane thought.

Important things are checked off en route, though.

Rufus is walked, fed and watered, left asleep before the fire in my study.

James is instructed to inform Marie that dinner needs to be delayed by an hour. If he thinks the request strange, or our haphazard state of dress, with beanies, scarves and coats askew, he doesn't even cock a brow.

And, unless the house is on fire, no one is to disturb us.

The second I have her across the threshold I kick the door closed and press her up against it. I can't get enough. Of her kisses, her moans, her body—just her, all her. Two weeks of denying myself this has tipped me into insanity, I swear.

'Is it locked?' She hurries out the words against my lips, her fingers tugging at my clothing.

'You think anyone is going to interrupt us after we specifically told them not to?'

She giggles, and the sound is like heaven in my already elated state. 'Good point.'

I thrust my coat to the floor, kick off my boots, all the while walking her backwards to the bed as she does the same. Hats, scarves, tops, trousers, socks, pants, bras—okay, just one bra!—are thrown aside, and then her burning skin is against mine.

'You feel so good...' I groan.

'So do you...' She leaps up, wraps her legs around my waist. 'Please tell me you have condoms now?'

I shake my head, kiss away her disappointed moan as I grip her thighs to me.

'But you said...?'

'I know what I said, but I was a fool. I trust you...if you trust me.'

'Of course.' She holds my face in her hands, stares into my eyes. 'Always.'

It's music to my desperate heart.

I can't believe I've kept my distance for so long. Feared the risk when the payoff is so great, so perfect. It's her, and she's everything. If she'll have me...lay down roots and commit.

Not that I'll say it aloud. Because even through the lustful haze I know she isn't ready to hear it. Not yet.

And so I stay quiet. Tell her with every sweep

of my lips, my tongue, my fingers how I feel, what I want and what I dream of for the future.

I know there's a clock ticking away somewhere. Her clock. The time she lives by.

But I'm done with dancing to its tune. I'm done with resisting this.

'Can I ask you something?' she says into the darkness some time later.

We're both spent and stuffed. Dinner in bed was her best idea yet, and once James got over the blushes it was dished out and cleared away with minimal fuss.

I press a kiss to her hair, pull her in closer as I stare unseeing at the ceiling. 'Anything.'

Because the truth is there's nothing I would keep from her. I'd lay my heart bare right now if I thought it would keep her here rather than make her run.

'Why me, do you think?'

'Besides the fact that you epitomise your name and I could no longer resist your smile?'

'Behave!' She gives me a little shove. 'I mean, why did Katherine choose me to inherit? Of all her foster children over the years, why me?'

'You said you'd read her letter.'

'I did, but…' She gives a tiny shrug. 'It's so much—too much.'

'She did it because she loved you.'

'She loved us all, Edward.'

I take a steady breath, knowing how brutal it will sound, but knowing I must tell her all the same…

'You were different, Summer. You didn't have anyone else.'

She presses away from me, her frown of confusion making my chest ache. 'Neither did the other children.'

I search her gaze. I don't want to hurt her. I don't want to push her away. I'm cherishing the closeness we've found, but it's so precious, so very new.

'Edward…?'

I force myself to put it into words, my arm still around her, holding her close. 'Gran fostered children who were hard to home, Summer. In a lot of cases she took siblings just so they could stay together and wouldn't be separated. But you…you were much older, and you had no siblings, but you were…you were flagged.'

She swallows. 'Flagged as being difficult?'

'Yes.'

'People didn't want me?'

The harsh truth spilling from her lips kills me and my arm pulses around her.

'I wanted you,' I say.

The words are fierce and from the very heart of me, giving me away, but she's too lost in her sadness to see it.

'Katherine did too.'

Her smile is so sad and I return it, my hand soft on her cheek as I sweep a stray tear from her skin.

'She did. She didn't care about all the homes you'd been through. She only cared about giving you this one. She wanted to be the parent who... who...' My voice chokes as her lower lip trembles, her lashes lowering to hide further tears from me.

'She wanted to be the one who saved me?' she whispers.

'Yes.' It's barely audible as I stroke her hair and press a kiss to her head, lift her chin so she will look at me and see the truth in my gaze. 'She chose you because she wanted you to come back home again.'

Her glistening blue eyes hold mine. 'She wanted you to come home too.'

'I know.'

I don't state the obvious. That Gran wanted us to make a home together, to be a real family...

I don't know what Gran's letter to Summer said, but surely she must know her true intentions. That whatever Gran had seen back then, whatever she'd seen in the intervening years, she believed we belonged together.

But this was Summer. Summer who'd never truly felt loved as a child. Her own mother had rejected her, then the system had failed her for a decade, tossing her back and forth foster homes, more and more rejection... Until Gran. Until Glenrobin.

How could I have threatened her with taking it away?

You were sitting on a twenty-year-old hurt. You felt betrayed by your grandmother. You were grieving and confused.

But does that justify how I've treated her?

I don't know.

I know I need to fix things now, though.

'This place will be your home for however long you want it to be, Summer.'

'You can't promise me that.'

'I can.'

She shakes her head, pushes against my hand to hide her eyes from me. To hide herself from me.

'One day you'll want to settle down...make a home with someone,' she says into my chest. 'That someone won't want me around.'

You are that someone.

The words are burning a hole in my heart, desperate on my tongue.

'Never, Summer. That I can promise you.'

A scratching at the door breaks the heavy silence that descends, and she lifts her head. 'It's Rufus.'

She starts to rise and I pull her back gently. 'I'll get him.'

She smiles, but it slays me, her eyes are so haunted by the past.

'You know he sleeps with me every night?' she confesses, and I smile back at her.

Lucky Rufus.

'I've noticed.'

I open the door a crack and he immediately rushes in, making for the bed.

'Can he?' she asks.

I eye the pair of them. 'So long as there's room for me too.'

Now her grin is wide, happiness as golden as her hair all around her as she pats the bed and gives Rufus an excited, 'Come on, buddy!'

Up he jumps, immediately circling to find his spot.

'He has a thing for pinning my feet down. Doesn't matter if I'm lying, sitting or standing... he finds his way to get on top of them.'

I return to the bed, scratch his head with a murmured, 'I like your thinking, Rufus.'

His ears prick, his puppy-dog eyes blink up at me, and Summer, who's puffing up her pillow, pauses. 'What was that?'

'Nothing—nothing at all.' I give him a final pat. 'Night-night, buddy.'

She gives a tired chuckle.

'What's so funny?'

'You.'

I join her under the quilt and she scoots into my side, her naked warmth instantly soothing.

'Why?'

'You've picked up on my nickname for him.'

'I have?'

'Uh-huh. Buddy. Do you think he's gonna get confused?'

Rufus is cocking his head back and forth listening to our little exchange.

'I don't think so. No more than usual at any rate.'

She gives me a playful thrust of her behind. 'Oi! Don't be mean.'

'Mean?' I murmur against her ear, catching her lobe between my teeth and fighting every urge to trail my lips lower. 'Mean would be kicking him out so I can have my wicked way with you again.'

She gives a sleepy laugh that's cut short with a yawn. 'You're insatiable.'

'Are you complaining?'

'Never.'

'What about ten years from now, will you complain then?' I say it in the heat of the moment, the heat of the drowsy connection but as soon as the words leave my lips, I hold my breath, force my body to relax when all it wants to do is tense against her.

'You're so funny, Edward. I prefer you like this, you know. Don't change.'

She thinks I'm joking, only I'm not.

I know that now.

I want her. I love her. And I will do everything in my power to keep her.

Time is all I need to convince her that she wants the same. And, thanks to Gran, I have it in abundance.

CHAPTER THIRTEEN

Summer

'SUMMER!'

Edward's shout jerks me out of my nervous, excited brain fog. The ball is today. *Today!*

I'm just praying nothing goes wrong. But if his voice is any indication, something already has.

I burst from the bedroom just as he arrives and walks me straight back in again, swinging the door closed behind him.

I stare up at his face. He's sporting a deer caught in the headlights look and my hand goes to my neck on impulse. 'What's happened?'

He shakes his head, strides past me to the window, looks out at the driveway, strides back and then returns once more.

'What the hell are my parents doing here?'

Ohhh... I nip my lip, swallow back the nerves.

'James says you invited them?'

He looks at me now, his eyes pinning me with their accusation.

Another swallow. 'I did.'

'Why?'

'Because, like I told you, I used Katherine's plans as a basis.'

'And that included her *guest list*?'

'Katherine would never have excluded your mother from this, and I didn't want to either.'

'But…'

He rakes a hand through his hair just as his mother's voice rings through the entrance hall, demanding attention from the staff. I cringe a little, but I stand by my decision…even if it's now adding to my acute case of nervous belly.

'Why is it such a problem, Edward? There'll be lots of other people here and she's confirmed they're only staying for one night and then leaving again tomorrow. It's just twenty-four hours. And you did say a small part of you hoped that one day things might get better with your mother…isn't the ball as good a place to start as any?'

He's staring at me, his mouth hanging open, his eyes still wide.

'She's your mother, Edward, not an axe murderer.' I give an awkward laugh. 'I'm sure you can get through one evening together. And you can catch up with your father, too. By your own admission things are better between the two of you at least.'

He shakes his head. He looks ill. Beside himself ill. I step closer, surprised at the strength of his reaction.

'I'm sorry.' I reach for his hand. 'I should've told you.'

'Why didn't you?'

'Well, at first, I couldn't get you to listen to anything, and after… I don't know. I guess I didn't want you to talk me out of it.'

He studies me intently and I squeeze his fingers softly.

'It'll be okay.'

'I wish I had your confidence.'

'I'll lend you some of mine,' I tease softly, and it coaxes out the smallest of smiles.

'I'm worried about you.' He swallows. 'I'm worried about how she will take us.'

My lashes flutter over the word 'us'. Are we an 'us' now?

Well, you have been sleeping together for two weeks…

My stomach swoops…my pulse races.

But an 'us'?

What did you expect? It's not like you've been clear about where this is heading or where it isn't. And haven't you been content—deliriously happy, even?

I wet my lips, struggling to find the right words, but then he releases my hand and strides away, leaving a ghostly chill in his place.

'We're hosting this party together. At Glenrobin, Summer.' He forks his fingers through his hair without looking at me. 'Rubbing my mother's face in the inheritance this early on feels like a risky move.'

And just like that the chill and the tension dissipates. He's not talking about our relationship. He's talking about our joint ownership of the estate.

"'Hell hath no fury like a woman scorned,'" he murmurs, and I stride up to him, confident that on this we're OK.

'I can handle your mother, Edward.'

He turns and reaches out to cup my cheek, his eyes tormented as they search mine. 'If she hurts you, Summer... If she says anything, I swear to God...'

My ribs ache, my heart swells. Would he have said something back then if he'd witnessed what she'd done, what she'd said...?

I mimic his touch, palm to cheek. 'And if she hurts you, Edward, or says anything, I swear to God...'

And then I kiss him. I kiss him with my gratitude, kiss him with my assurance that I can look after myself, kiss him until the world beyond this room no longer exists.

'You know,' he says against my lips, 'a wise person once said to me that the best form of stress relief can be found between the sheets.'

I squeal as he scoops me up and makes for the bed, rousing a sleeping Rufus, who shifts just in time for our arrival. 'And let me guess...that wise person was Juan?'

'How did you know?'

I laugh as he covers me with his body, turn my

head from his approaching kiss… 'Isn't it rude to keep our guests waiting?'

'I shall explain we were otherwise engaged…' he teases my earlobe between his teeth '…with last-minute planning and preparations, of course.'

'I'm loving your thinking…' I tug his sweater over his head, my eyes roving hungrily over him.

'And I'm loving yours.'

Edward

I check my watch for the umpteenth time. She's not late. I'm early. Early and eager and…

I adjust my cravat.

'Will you stop that?' Marie bats my hands away. 'Every time you wiggle it, you ruin the symmetry.'

'The *symmetry*?' I raise my brows at her. 'I'm wearing frills and you're worrying about the symmetry?'

'Nonsense!' She pats her curly white wig that is sprinkled with glitter and waves her fairy god-mother wand at me. 'You look very prince-like, and that colour becomes you.'

I look down at the navy satin brocade jacket with its gold trim and grimace. Bad enough that the trousers feel more like tights—breeches, I've been assured—but the floral pattern woven through the jacket and waistcoat…not to mention the satin shirt…

'You know, you're so sexy when you get like this.'

'Like what?'

'Inspired. Passionate.'

'I'll remind you of that on the day.'

'What day?'

'The day of the ball...when you see your costume.'

Our conversation in the snow comes back to me, and just like that I'm smiling. Smiling and remembering her teasing and her promise to play the role. My damsel in distress.

As if.

'Oh, my!'

Marie gasps, her hand over her mouth, as she looks past me. And I know what she's seen—or rather who. Her presence thickens the very air that I breathe, my body warms, and slowly I turn, lift my gaze to the top of the grand staircase, and there she is.

Summer.

Her name resonates through me as my vision narrows and she's all I can see. Her golden hair tumbling free about her bare shoulders...a dusting of sparkle all over...her iridescent dress the colour of the mist that enshrouds Glenrobin on the most mystical of days.

Ethereal. Magical. Otherworldly. She could have stepped out of a fairy tale herself.

And isn't that the point?

Tonight she is a true princess and she's mine. All mine.

Marie gives a soft chuckle beside me. 'Best close that mouth of yours before you catch a fly, Master Edward.'

I choke my agreement. Do as she suggests. But there's no moving—my feet are rooted. I'm incapable of anything but watching as Summer lifts the layers of tulle enough to reveal silver stilettos on her feet and starts to descend.

The light of the chandelier plays across her skin, her dress…over the silver-stitched pattern of birds and butterflies in the skirt and the heart-shaped corset that's a work of art. Its fairy tale scene is so detailed that I want to trace it with my fingers, every millimetre of it—and her.

She gives me a coy smile as she reaches the bottom step—a smile that is so unlike her it makes my heart flip and my hand reach out on impulse. 'Prince Charming at your service, Princess.'

I bow my head but keep my eyes fixed on hers, and her smile grows, stealing my breath and my heart with it.

'I think it's Cinders,' she whispers, slipping her hand into mine.

'Not on my watch.'

I'm vaguely aware that Marie has left us. Vaguely aware that there's a reason why I can't pull her to me and kiss her as deeply as I'd like.

I raise her hand to my lips, sweep her knuckles with the briefest kiss. 'You look breathtaking.'

She wets her glossy lips. 'You scrub up pretty well too.'

I smile. The look in her eye is worth every frill and every revealing inch below my waist. 'Are you ready to greet your guests?'

She gives an unsteady laugh. 'I want to be. But of all the things I've done, this has to be the most terrifying.'

'Come now, Princess…' I encourage her down the last step and place her hand on my arm. 'You've travelled the globe, faced challenges I can barely imagine. You've built classrooms and homes with your bare hands. You've taught English to women when their communities would have had them bearing babies instead. You've protested for women's rights and been imprisoned for it. You, my darling, have no need to be afraid.'

She's staring up at me, her eyes reaching wider and wider with every word. 'You really have been reading up on me.'

Reading up on you, devouring your postcards, falling in love with you…yes, that's me.

'When the subject is so fascinating, how could I stop?'

'Edward…' She shakes her head in wonder, her lips pursed, her eyes shining.

'Now, if I'm not mistaken that is the sound of the first guests arriving, and although James is dressed to receive—thank you for also putting him in breeches, by the way, I'm not sure I could have done this alone—I think it's customary for us to be at the door too.'

'Of course. But your parents…will they want to join us?'

I give a short laugh. 'My mother likes to make an entrance. She'll be fashionably late—which gives us plenty of time to enjoy your efforts before she tries to taint them.'

Her eyes tighten, her smile too. 'She might surprise you.'

'She might.'

But she won't.

I tried to speak to my mother earlier, to warn her to be on best behaviour, but she wouldn't even deign to speak to me. Too busy getting ready was the excuse she gave. Avoiding me, more like.

I can only hope that an audience of the rich and powerful, not to mention the great British press, will do what my undelivered threat couldn't.

I can hope, but not even the sight of Summer's unparalleled beauty can ease the prickle of unease at the base of my spine.

I didn't miss the panic flaring in her gaze when I referred to there being an 'us'. I backtracked well enough, using the inheritance as my cover, but she gave herself away so clearly and I'm worried.

This relationship we've built is far too fragile, far too new, and one barbed comment from my mother could see it crumbling to the ground. And I'm not ready for this to be over…nowhere near.

Summer

The evening is everything I dreamed of and more.

The look of wonder in the eyes of the guests as they take it all in—the ice sculptures, the hand-carved pumpkins, the autumnal decorations that lead them to explore each fairy tale scene in its own little nook... The adults are loving it as much as the children, and with all the compliments they shower me with, the gratitude too, I *feel* like a princess.

Me. Summer from the wrong side of the tracks. Holding court with my handsome Prince...

I giggle with the craziness of it.

'What now?' Edward groans as he spins us around the dance floor to an old classic. The soft light of the candelabra and the fairy lights add to the sparkle in his rich brown eyes.

'What do you mean, what now?'

'That laugh... An hour ago it was because my breeches were giving me grief. I can't bear thinking what it might be now...'

'You'll laugh at me.'

'Right now, I feel like you're laughing at *me*—again—so have at it.'

'If you must know I was laughing at the fact I actually feel like a princess.'

His grin lights me up inside. 'Enjoy it. You deserve every royal second.'

'I had a lot of help.'

'This is all you, Summer.' His eyes turn serious, his arm around my waist pulling me closer. 'What you've managed to create, the world you've built…'

He gestures to the room around us. Kids and adults alike are all dancing, talking, laughing, racing between the fairy tale scenes, raiding the dress-up boxes, creating pictures in the photo booths… Everyone is happy.

'You took Gran's vision and made it your own. Just look at the fun around you. As for the donations—I have it on good authority you're going to break Gran's record and then some.'

'I just want to do her proud.'

'You've—'

'It's so juvenile! I don't even know why we agreed to come, do you?'

That voice pierces the music…pierces me and I stumble mid-step. If it wasn't for Edward's grip, I would have face-planted for all the world to see.

Okay, so not everyone is happy.

He sweeps me past the bystanders, but his posture is as rigid as mine. I know he heard her too. I wet my lips, glance up, but he's not looking at me. His eyes are on his mother and projecting fire and ice in one.

'Edward, it's okay.'

'It isn't okay,' he says between his teeth.

'Please, I don't want a scene. Like you say, it's

a success—a huge success. The auction went far better than I could ever hope for.'

'The auction *she* didn't even participate in.'

'Did you really expect her to? Besides…she at least made the effort to dress up.'

'Dress up?'

'Yes. Do you think she knew who we were going to be when she chose the evil stepmother get-up?'

He laughs against me, the tension easing from his body. 'You know that's no costume, right?'

I blink up at him in mock innocence. 'Are you serious? But it's all black and angular—and, frankly, quite scary.'

'Ah, don't worry, Princess…' He leans in, whispers beside my ear, and a thrilling shiver runs right through me. 'I'll protect you.'

'Lucky me.' It's as breathless as I feel.

'Lucky you, indeed.'

He twirls us further away, but I can't help bringing the focus back to her. 'Have you spoken to her yet?'

The tension ripples through him again and I bite my lip. Maybe I should leave well alone—but she's still his mother. Still his blood. Though I should know better than most that blood means nothing.

'We exchanged pleasantries…once she deemed herself ready for me. I think I came after Charles but before the caterers.'

He's teasing, and I hate it that he feels he must tease about something so hurtful.

'Actually, poor Charles had something of an ear-bashing about the inheritance, so I was forced to step in.'

'Oh, God, poor man.'

'Don't worry—he can hold his own when it comes to my mother's viperous tongue. I take it she hasn't spoken to you yet?'

I give a choked scoff, try to brush off the sting of it. 'Clearly I'm beneath the caterers.'

'You're the hostess of Glenrobin's event of the year. It has nothing to do with society's hierarchy and everything to do with the fact she can't see past her own bitterness.'

I grimace. 'I really did make things worse, didn't I?'

'You did what you thought was right.'

'But *you* were right. It's too soon. I shouldn't have invited her. I should have given her more time to come to terms with everything.'

'I don't know, Summer… Excluding her would have made her angry, too. You can't win.'

I search his eyes, see the truth of it and feel the sadness it brings. 'Just like Katherine couldn't…'

'Hey, don't let her spoil tonight. This is on her, not you.'

I can't bring myself to agree.

'I mean it, Princess…' He bows his head, brushes the lightest kiss to my ear. 'Forget about her and enjoy your ball, because everyone else who matters is.'

I let my gaze drift over the room, catch sight of Juan at the bar, surrounded by a group of attentive women, and manage a smile. 'Your friend certainly is.'

He follows my line of sight. 'It never takes him long to garner an audience.'

'He does have a certain something about him.'

Edward's eyes come back to me, sharp, probing. 'Don't tell me you go in for that tall, dark and handsome thing?'

'Oh, I don't know…his Spanish can be quite the aphrodisiac.'

He's jealous—it's as obvious as the warmth radiating off his body into mine. And provoking him is sending me a little dizzy.

'As for the tall, dark, and handsome thing…it certainly appeals. But I prefer mine quintessentially British.'

I stroke the base of his neck as I let my meaning hit home and feel rather than hear the soft growl that he gives. 'You'd better believe it, Princess.'

My laugh is breathy. 'You know, I could get used to that.'

'What?'

'You calling me Princess.'

'Stick around long enough and I'll call you it all you like.'

My heart pulses with the vehemence in his

tone—but he's teasing, right? So why does it feel like a proposition of sorts? A demand? A desire for this to be something more…?

But how much more?

I press my cheek to his chest, hide my eyes from his and lose myself in the dance, the music, and the steady beat of his heart beneath my ear.

His mother continues to hover on the outskirts, like an annoying gnat that keeps buzzing, close enough to be heard but not close enough to take out. Not that I'd dare.

And she's hurting too…in her own way. She's lost her mother and what would have been her home.

As for me—I'm not that scared teenager trying to find a place in a world that doesn't make sense, running away from her cutting words. I can hold my ground… Although that doesn't mean I belong here, with her son, any more than I did back then.

For now, though, I snuggle in closer, let his warmth ease away the chill. For now, I can hold on to this feeling and get through tonight and tomorrow and the next day…until the day comes when I have to say goodbye.

'Are you ready to give your speech?' he asks.

I press away from his chest. 'Not particularly. Public speaking isn't really my forte.'

'You'll be fine.'

'Are you sure I can't persuade you into giving it?'

'I'm going to present you, but this amazing achievement is all you, and I'm not stealing your glory.'

His encouragement teases out a smile. 'Well, when you put it like that...'

He leads me towards the band, releases me with a gentle squeeze of his fingers. I watch as he negotiates ownership of the microphone and the flutters inside me multiply.

You can do this, I silently tell myself. *Just speak from the heart—that's all you need to do. Tell them your truth and be thankful.*

Thankful.

I can do that.

Edward's talking. The music has stopped, the chatter in the room too. The waiting staff are handing out glasses of champagne and everyone is listening to Edward's deep, resonating tone. And then he's looking right at me, his hand reaching out...

'Ladies and gentlemen, Princesses and Princes, Knights and—'

'Fairies!' a little girl shouts, and he chuckles.

'And fairies... Please put your hands together for the woman who made all this possible: Summer Evans.'

I step towards him, accepting a glass of champagne from a passing waitress on autopilot.

'Do fetch me the sick bucket, Rupert.'

My step falters, my fingers tremble around the glass.

Ignore her...she's just acting out...don't look...

'Hush, darling, people will hear.'

'You think I care?'

I tighten my hold on my drink and drown out Edward's parents with the look in his eye. The warmth, the admiration...

Camera flashes go off as I take the microphone and I'm reminded of the press there amongst the masses.

'You've got this,' he whispers in my ear as I take his place and plaster on the biggest, warmest of smiles.

'Thank you, my Prince.'

I swear I hear his mother scoff, but I can't really—not from this distance. I take in my audience and focus on the children...focus on the child I once was...

'Thank you all for coming.' I raise my glass in salute. 'When I took on this challenge a month ago, I have to be honest, I wasn't sure I could pull it off. But Katherine's name opened a lot of doors, just as she opened many of our hearts—including mine. I also had her encouraging voice in my ear, telling me I could do anything I set my mind to. There weren't many people willing to take on the challenge I presented as a child, but she did. She welcomed me into her home, gave me a safe space to live, to learn, to love and to grow. She believed her purpose in life was to give to others what they otherwise wouldn't have—to help children become the best possible version of themselves. Without her, I don't know where I'd be now…'

A scuffle to my left draws my attention, but I can't see through the spotlight that's been placed on me. I'm very much centre stage, and Edward's vanished.

I hurry on before my silence draws attention. 'To have this opportunity now, to continue Katherine's good work, in her name, means the absolute world. And I don't say that lightly. Thank you so much for your generosity this evening—your donations have surpassed our highest hopes. To the band, the caterers, the staff…thank you for such an amazing evening. This Princess couldn't be prouder. And to all the guests, kids and adults alike, please continue to enjoy the evening. It is our absolute pleasure to entertain you here at Glenrobin. May we do this all again next year! To the children!'

I raise my glass to the crowd and they do the same to me, their cheers resounding off the walls…

Wow. I breathe it all in and know the moment will stay with me for ever.

I return the microphone to the band leader, and when I turn back people are rushing forward to talk to me, to thank me, to congratulate me. It's fabulous, wonderful, but where's Edward? I want him by my side. I want him to share in this.

A reporter steps forward. 'Miss Evans? How about a photo of you with some of the children?'

'Yes. Yes. Of course.'

But I'm scanning the crowd, peering through the gaps and over the heads. And then I see him. With his parents. His mother's animated, her face full of colour, her eyes blazing even from across the distance, and Edward...

If looks could kill.

'Just here, Miss Evans.'

'Huh?'

It's the reporter, gesturing to where she has a few of the kids gathered, all with excited grins and a definite sugar-high shining in their faces.

'Of course...sorry.'

I hurry to their side, all smiles and encouragement, but my heart races in a panicked staccato, and my eyes are trying to keep abreast of Edward and his parents while also performing for the children and the camera.

'Now, if you'll all just face me and smile...'

It's then that his mother slaps him. One deft crack across his cheek. And I swear the room freezes, my blood runs cold. Cold, but hot. Hot with rage.

How *dare* she?

She might be hurting, but—

'Miss Evans? Miss Evans...?'

I blink, refocus. The journalist is talking to me, the music is still playing, people are talking. I look back to Edward, but all I see is his exiting form, steering his mother firmly from the room, his father trailing behind.

I look back to where they were standing. No one else seems to have noticed. In fact, most eyes are trained on me and the children, having our picture taken...

And if you don't start performing soon, they'll know something's amiss.

I force my grin wide. 'Let's try that again, shall we, kids?'

I crouch down to their level and pull them in for a hug. I have a job to do. I'm the Princess and this ball is for them... I can deal with the evil stepmother in due course.

And deal with her, I will.

If Katherine's wake-up call wasn't enough, she's about to get another...with both barrels.

CHAPTER FOURTEEN

Edward

'Do YOU REALLY want to make a scene in front of the press, Mother? Are you out of your mind?'

'Look, son…'

My father tries to come between us but I'm almost past caring. A red haze has descended and I'm ready to throw her out through the door, snow and all.

'I don't think this is going to help.'

'*Help?*' I don't even look at him. My fury is one hundred percent directed at my mother. 'What kind of person accepts an invitation to a ball that is all about raising money for underprivileged children and behaves like you have? Looking down your nose at everything, constantly bitching, with a complete disregard for the work that has gone into this night…'

'The *work*? The money, you mean. *My* money.'

'It was never your money.' The words vibrate with my anger.

'It should have been. Just as all of this should have been.'

'Come now, darling—'

'Will you shut up, Rupert? He needs to hear this.' She rounds on me, her fury filling my study.

'You think some silly inheritance means that girl belongs in your world? Seeing you both together, canoodling on the dance floor…it's an embarrassment, Edward, an utter disgrace.'

'You're the disgrace, Mother.'

She moves to strike me again, but this time I'm quicker and I grasp her wrist before she can make contact, throw it down.

'Why don't you try that on someone your own size?'

All heads snap to the doorway as Summer strides through it and I bite back a curse. I'd hoped by extricating my mother from the ballroom I could save Summer from further upset…instead she's walked straight into the firing line.

'I'm not even going to lower myself to speak to *you*,' my mother spits. 'An upstart who can have nothing to say that's worth listening to.'

'Mother, I'm warning you—'

'Edward, it's okay.' Summer presses a hand to my chest, all gentle, but her eyes are on fire. 'I've got this.'

She turns to face my mother and I watch my mother's nostrils flare; Summer's strength and dignity in the face of her wrath only serving to rile her further.

'This "upstart" may not have been born into money, or had the greatest start in life,' she says smoothly, 'but thanks to Katherine I've made something of it and helped people along the way.

I'm proud of what I've achieved. Can you honestly say the same?'

'I— You…' my mother splutters, her puffed-out cheeks turning puce.

'You were born into money, Lady Fitzroy, and you married into a title too. What have you done with it?'

My mother's mouth flaps like a fish but nothing comes out.

'Precisely.'

Oh, God, I want to laugh. She has the woman hung, drawn and quartered with barely a word spoken. She has more of Gran in her than my mother can ever hope to.

'Now, you listen here…'

My mother takes a threatening step towards her, and I'm so in awe of Summer that I'm a second too late to step in. But my father is there, his hand on my mother's arm, his eyes flashing in warning.

'That's enough, Carina.'

Summer hasn't even flinched. 'I'm not saying this to be cruel, Lady Fitzroy. I'm saying it because you need a wake-up call.'

'*I* need a wake-up call! A bit rich coming from you, don't you think?'

'Actually, no. I think I'm best placed to tell you so.'

'*You?*' she sneers. 'A girl who's come into an inheritance that she doesn't deserve, acting above her station? I don't think so. This is ludicrous—this whole situation. I don't even know why I'm standing here speaking to you. You take my mother's attention when she's alive, and now you take her home in her death. It's unbelievable.'

'Mother, I've already warned you!'

But Summer's hand is back on my chest, soothing me, reassuring me.

'The truth is, this house would have been yours, Lady Fitzroy, if you'd returned an ounce of the love Katherine tried to give you over the years. All she ever tried to do was make it up to you. For the way her parents ostracised you both. The way she was barely more than a child when she had you, scared and alone. She tried, but all you were interested in was taking. Financially, not emotionally.'

My mother is stunned and still, and Summer has us all captive.

'It won't have been an easy decision for her to make, but she wanted to provide me with a home. She wanted Edward to have the same. She loved him, and she was proud of him—his achievements, his good heart. The fact he possesses all of those in spite of the way you treat him is some kind of miracle. And she hoped that one day you would see sense and return to Glenrobin as his loving mother and not...' Summer nips her lip, her cheeks flushing just a little '...not as you are now. I didn't invite you to rub your nose in my good fortune, as you see it—'

'Like hell you didn't,' my mother scoffs, but Summer's unperturbed.

'I invited you because this whole night is in memory of your mother and co-hosted by your son. You belong here.' She tilts her chin up. 'But now you've outstayed your welcome. I'd appreciate it if you packed your things and left. I don't want bad press to taint what has been a lovely evening, and I certainly don't want the kids to witness the kind of violence you displayed in the ballroom.'

'Don't you— Why, you—? Rupert! Edward! Are you really going to stand there and let her speak to me like that?'

I have to smother the grin that wants to crack my face in two. I have never seen my mother so unsettled, or Summer so utterly empowered and stunning with it. My chest swells with pride as my heart pounds with my love for her. If I could sweep her up into a kiss and ravish her senseless, I would.

Definitely not what my mother is asking me to do…

There's a rap on the door and James steps in. 'Lord and Lady Fitzroy's car is ready.'

'Thank you, James.' Summer sends him the most dazzling smile and folds her hands in front of her. 'Now, if you please…?'

My mother blows out a flustered breath, looks from me to my father and back again, but neither of us are moving.

She pins Summer with her frosty stare. 'You haven't heard the end of this, you foolish woman.'

And then she's off, storming out of the room.

'At least I've progressed from being the "foolish child" I was, Lady Fitzroy,' Summer calls after her.

I frown over the reference. Foolish child? Summer's tone resonates with meaning. Did my mother once call her that? All those years ago?

'I'm sorry, son,' my father says into the sudden silence. 'She's confused. Things have been a little odd since Katherine fell ill and—'

'It doesn't excuse her behaviour tonight.'

'No…no, of course not. But—please don't write her off for good.'

My nod is very slight, because I can't make that promise. It hinges so much on my mother, and she's too unpredictable. She could have ruined everything tonight. If not for Summer's courage, her strength, her performance just now, I'd be convinced she had.

'Miss Evans…'

My father turns to Summer, his respectful form of address taking her by surprise, judging by the way her brows lift. Hell, it surprises me too.

'If you will permit me to speak openly?'

She nods. 'Of course.'

He smiles his gratitude. 'I will admit I had my doubts when I heard the news regarding your inheritance. And it came as a huge shock to my wife—which I'm sure you can understand. There was no forewarning. And, if I'm honest, Carina hasn't come to terms with Katherine's death. Their relationship was always strained at best, but that's not to say she doesn't feel her loss or mourn what might have been. I know you thought the worst when she refused to return for the reading of the will, Edward. But if you'd seen her lately you'd know how much she's struggling… Anyway, I digress—and I'm making excuses again, I know. But what I wanted to say—'

'Rupert!' my mother hollers from the hall, and I pray that most of the guests are still ensconced in the ballroom and distracted by the music.

My father spares the doorway the briefest of glances before coming back to Summer and taking her hand in both of his. 'You have done Glenrobin and my wife's family so very proud tonight, Miss Evans. Katherine obviously saw in you what some of us missed…to our own detriment, might I add.' He gives me an odd look. 'But I see great things in Glenrobin's future with you and my son at the helm, and I wish you every success with your charity ventures. If there is anything I can do to help, please don't hesitate to call.'

Summer blinks…blinks again. Like me, she can't believe her ears—her eyes, even. My father looks moved to tears. Hell, *I'm* moved to tears.

'Right, I'd best go. I think your mother's going

to need some talking down—or a talking-to. Maybe it's high time for the latter.'

I *think* he's teasing, but after tonight's turn of events I can't be sure.

He places his hand on my shoulder. 'Let's get together soon for a drink, son. It's been too long.'

I clear my throat, nod.

'Goodnight to you both.'

And with that he walks away, leaving us staring after him.

Dumbfounded doesn't even come close.

But a flicker of excitement comes alive inside me—a surge of emotion that builds and builds as I recall the whole scene… The way Summer stood up to my mother, the way she defended me, talked about me, the way she acted.

Is she finally ready to accept her place here?

To accept that she belongs?

And not just temporarily…

The future fills with possibility—marriage, children, family…a true home in every sense of the word. Everything Gran wished for.

I can't breathe for the excited rush I feel, and as she turns to me, her blue eyes so bright, her cheeks so flushed…

'Wow!' she breathes, her hands on her hips as she gives a rapid shake of her head. 'Did that just happen?'

'Sure did, Princess.' I reach out and tug her to me. 'You were incredible.'

'Not too much?'

'No, definitely not too much.'

'It's just that when I saw her strike you in the ballroom, I was ready to give her both barrels.'

I wince. 'You saw that?'

She nods, her eyes sad as she strokes her finger over my smarting cheek. 'I pondered dragging her out by her hair and telling the children it was all part of the entertainment, but then I'd have been lowering myself to her level.'

'Now, that would have been a sight to witness—but you're right. What you did was far more powerful.'

'You reckon?'

'There's no doubt in my mind that your words had a greater impact.'

'I hope so, Edward, I truly do.'

'I couldn't stand it any longer—the snide little comments, the digs…'

'I know. She needs to realise she's brought this on herself. I came in here determined to make her see why Katherine did what she did, and how different things could have been—how different things could *still* be—if she saw the error of her ways, but I don't know… Has it gone in? Any of it?'

'You've done all you can. So has Gran, so have I. The rest is up to her.'

'I think a good counsellor wouldn't go amiss.'

'Baby steps, Princess.'

'Maybe your father could take on that battle?'

'Maybe. But tell me something: what did you mean when you told her you'd progressed from being a foolish child?'

She falters before me and I know she wishes I hadn't asked. But I had to. I had to know...

'Did my mother call you that?'

She swallows, hooks her arms around my neck. 'Do we have to talk about her any more? Can't we just—?'

'Summer...tell me.'

Her lashes flutter and I lose her gaze to the past...some memory she's never disclosed...

'Do you remember the last time we saw one another?'

I frown. 'Of course. It was the day of the Christmas party. We'd been helping prepare the presents and you'd left to get ready. But then you never showed up.'

'I showed up.' Her throat bobs. 'I saw you at the party.'

'But—but Gran said you had a headache, that you'd gone to bed.'

She wets her lips. 'Heartache, more like.'

Heartache...

My stomach twists, my frown deepens. 'But I don't—'

'I was there, Edward. I saw you with Charlotte and your mother saw me. She took great delight in pointing out my inadequacies, and the fact that I would never stack up to her…'

'To who? My mother?'

'No. To Charlotte. Though I guess in hindsight she meant both.'

'But there was never anything between Charlotte and me. She was simply the daughter of one of my mother's friends. We never shared anything more than polite pleasantries at social functions.'

'I… I didn't know that. And your mother…well, she noticed the way I was looking at you and saw fit to intervene and put me in my place.'

My heart pulses. 'The way you were looking at me?'

'Apparently my feelings for you were written in my face.'

Oh, God. I can scarcely breathe, let alone speak. 'Your *feelings*?'

She nods.

'What are you saying, Summer?'

'That once upon a time this teen dared to believe in her own fairy tale and fancied herself in love with the Prince.'

I wet my lips. 'You mean me?'

She doesn't confirm or deny, and I feel I've lost her wholly to the past now.

'Your mother took the opportunity to save me the humiliation of a public rejection. She likely thought I'd be grateful.'

'My God, Summer, she had no right! Why

didn't you come to me? Why weren't you honest with me?'

'Because I was scared, and I was weak, and your mother had only confirmed everything I believed back then.'

'*She* was the reason you left?' I choke out.

All that pain, all that wasted time—*two decades!*—because my mother couldn't keep her mouth shut.

'And still you're trying to help her?'

'No, Edward. I might have thought she was the reason back then. A month ago, even. But the truth is *I'm* the reason I left. She only brought my departure forward; I would have left eventually. We both know that.'

I stare at her. Unable to believe it…not wanting to believe it. Much preferring to blame my mother for my heartache than the woman I've never stopped loving…

But was she right? Back then, would she have left anyway, to pursue all those adventures, all those charity expeditions? Would she have kept on running for fear of being rejected, like her mother and so many foster parents had rejected her before?

I can't deny it's possible.

But not now.

Things are different.

She's different.

I know that, having witnessed her tonight, this past month…

Surely now she can see how worthy she is and how perfect our life could be if we walk it together…follow the path Gran forged and make it our own.

I know I need to lay my heart bare—that it's the only way to make her see. And then our life together can start in earnest. No more wasting time, no more doubt.

'Perhaps. But what of now, Summer? What of the future?'

Summer

He looks serious. More serious than I've ever seen him. And he wants to talk about the future…

'The future?' I say…wary, unsure.

'Don't you see?' Passion heats his words, and his chocolate eyes are molten. 'If you stay here you can carry all this on. You can keep Glenrobin at the heart of the community. Use the estate, its wealth, its connections, to give back on another scale. There is so much more you could do…so much heart you have to give, Summer. You and Gran came from very different backgrounds, but you have no idea how similar you are. And with your childhood, your insight into what it's like…'

My childhood, my background…

I swallow down the feeling of inferiority, because in Edward's eyes I'm no less for any of it. He's trying to tell me I belong here—and, hell, didn't I feel it? Standing up against his mother. Feeling that sense of belonging deep in my bones.

But for how long? How long before he peels away the layers and realises I'm not worthy of his attentions, his praise, his love…? Because that's what I see in his eyes right now, and I don't want to stick around and see that light go out.

'You could take these charity efforts to the next level, Summer. Go national—international, even.'

I give a heady laugh. 'And there I was thinking you'd caution me into walking before running.'

'Not when you're as capable as you are.'

For a second I lose myself in that look, those words. Feel his warmth, his encouragement, his passion seeping beneath my skin, heating my heart, making me want so much more than I can ever possibly have.

'Now you're just trying to big me up after your mother's attack, but I don't need you to.' I try and dismiss it all. 'I'm fine.'

'I *know* you're fine. That's not what this is about.'

'No?'

He stares at me long and hard, with something desperate in his gaze, and then he parts his lips and I hold my breath.

'I love you, Summer.'

'You…' My voice dies, my gut rolls, my heart—Hell, I don't want to think about my heart.

'Did you hear me, Summer? I love you!'

The air rushes from my lungs, his confession ricocheting through my body—very real, very much heard. I shake my head…shake it again as my arms fall away.

'Don't say that.'

He frowns at me. 'Why, when it's the truth?'

'You can't love me!'

He gives a strained laugh. 'I'm afraid that ship's sailed.'

'No, Edward, you don't understand. No one can love me. There's something wrong with me. Not even my own flesh and blood loved me! Not even people who'd committed their lives to helping people like me could love me! How can you possibly even *begin* to love me?'

'Oh, baby, baby, baby…'

He tries to pull me to him but I back away and he blanches, his eyes pained and so full of sorrow. For me.

'How can you not see how incredible you are?' he asks.

I want to press my hands to my ears, block out his words and the sickness rising inside me.

'You lived through a nightmare childhood and still you smiled, still you cared. You were so full of sunshine and laughter. And, hell, you were a nightmare, too. A hellion with a chip on her shoulder. But you kicked the attitude and kept all the charm. You could have gone down that dark road and kept on walking, but you didn't. How could I not fall in love with you?'

'But you didn't—you never—not back then... not really...'

I wave a shaky hand at him. He can't be saying that he loved me then. Fancied me, sure. Loved me as a friend, absolutely. But more than that?

'You had girls flocking around you...girls who belonged in your world. You had Charlotte, and she was so right for you.'

'So right for my mother, maybe, and what she wanted for me. But she wasn't you and I wanted *you*. To hell with what my mother told you. I only kept it from you because I was scared of taking advantage. You were young, vulnerable, mixed-up, I didn't want to make things worse for you.'

My whole body trembles. 'This is crazy, ridiculous...'

'No, what's ridiculous is you rejecting my love for you...my dreams for a future with you. The future that Gran so clearly wanted for us.'

'Don't bring Katherine into this.'

'At the risk of sounding like a child...' the hint of a spark reaches his eyes '...she started it and now I intend to finish it. I'm done with being afraid, Summer. I want to make Glenrobin a family home again. For *us*.'

'Please, Edward...please, don't do this. Don't spoil this moment, this night, with heartfelt promises that—that can't stand the test of time.'

'It's a declaration of love, Summer.'

'Love is fickle, Edward.'

His frown deepens. 'But that's where you're wrong. I loved you twenty years ago and you left before I could tell you. I'm not making that same mistake again.'

'Edward, please…you're upset after what happened with your mother…you're shocked at your father's kindness.'

I turn away. I can't bear the pain in his eyes as I reject him. Because the heart *is* weak. It is changeable. It's why I always run before it has a chance to change on me.

My mother taught me that.

Foster homes taught me that.

Run before you're pushed.

Run before you suffer the pain of rejection.

Run because that is in your control.

'I'm all of those things, Summer—upset, shocked…disconcerted, even. But it doesn't change how I feel about you. It doesn't change the fact that I love you and I always will.'

What blood is left in my face drains completely. My heart tries to fight its way to the surface, tries to cherish his words. To hell with the fear, to protecting myself…

I start to pace, desperate to keep moving, desperate to force it all out…the confusion, the shock, the temptation. 'You're upset…you don't know what you're saying…you can't…'

'I'm forty-two, Summer. Credit me with enough maturity to know my own mind and what is in my own heart. So when I say I love you and I want to marry you, I mean it.'

'Let's just pretend this didn't happen,' I ramble on, acting as if I haven't heard him—although I have, every word brands my well-bitten heart. 'We shouldn't have started sleeping in the same bed every night. It was bound to blur things… confuse what this is and what it isn't. Stupid, *stupid* woman.'

I slap my forehead and he moves to stop me. I leap out of his reach.

'What the hell were you thinking? You've ruined everything!' I rub my face. It's damp. And I can't catch my breath through the sobs racking my body.

'Summer, stop and breathe. Just breathe.'

I shake my head, shake it more, my eyes wide as I refuse to look at him—not that I can see through the tears.

'Look at me, Summer. *Look at me.*'

He reaches out, gently clasps my wrists to pull me round to face him, his expression so earnest, his brown eyes ablaze.

'You've done nothing wrong; *we've* done nothing wrong.'

I wet my lips, but I can't put words to my deepest fear. My mother's rejection almost broke me—a

wound that Katherine helped to heal. But Edward...
Edward's rejection would tear me in two.

And there'd be no fix for that.

'Tell me you don't love me, Summer. Tell me
you don't feel the same.'

'I can't do this, Edward,' I sob out. 'I can't.'

He rests his palm against my cheek, his thumb
sweeping away the tears that fall.

'Why? Why can't you love me?'

'I just can't.' My body shudders as I force it out.

'The thing is, Summer, you don't get a say in it.
Falling in love isn't something you can control. It
happens to you, and it changes you. It makes you
yearn to be with that person, to live your life with
that person, shape your life around them. That's
what I want—if you can let yourself want it too.'

I shake my head. Wanting it. Yearning for it.
That life...so full, so happy. And so very far to
fall...

'I can't...' I whisper, weaker but no less ada-
mant.

'Why? Because I'm not giving up until you explain it to me in terms that I can understand and
get on board with.'

I hold his eye and let my confession fall with
the tears. 'Because the day you stop loving me
will crush me.'

The faintest of smiles touches his lips. 'Oh,
baby, who says anything about stopping? I want

to love you for the rest of my days—that's what a real marriage is.'

'Want and doing are very different things.'

'They don't have to be.'

'You'll wake up one day and want me gone. Just like my mother. Just like all those foster parents…'

'Not Gran. She loved you from the moment she met you.'

'Because I left. Because I stayed away. Don't you see? If I'd tried to make a home here, eventually she'd have seen the real me. She'd have turned me away just like all the rest.'

He's shaking his head. 'You couldn't be more wrong.'

'Life has proved otherwise.'

'No, Summer. This doesn't have to end—not if we don't want it to.'

'All things end, Edward. It's a universal truth.'

'Yes, but we can choose that ending. And I'd rather go to my grave loving you than live the rest of my life without you.'

My body gravitates towards him, pleading for his warmth, his kiss, anything to fill the emptiness inside me.

'Open your heart to the possibility, Summer.'

'It hurts…'

'Life hurts. There are no certainties. I know that. But I also know that the hardest things in life—the things that hurt the most—do so because they're worth it. *You* are worth it. Don't turn your back on what we have out of fear.'

He lifts his other hand, cups my face in both as he looks into my eyes.

'Let me love you and make a future with you and prove you otherwise.'

And then he kisses me, and the world seems to settle. The ground beneath my feet solidifies, my heart calms…and then I'm transported back, standing in a cold corridor, Ted clutched in my hand, watching the woman I'd tried to be everything for walk away, and I'm shoving at his chest.

'No. No. *No*.' I can't breathe… I can't see. 'I can't do this. I *can't*.'

I race for the door, for the back of the house, away from the guests, the press, and the ball still underway. I break out into the garden and the cold wraps around me, invades me.

But it's not enough.

I don't want to feel any more. I want the heat of his touch off my skin. The heat of his words out of my heart. I need to escape. I need to be free.

I need it to be just me.

Safe. Known. Protected.

CHAPTER FIFTEEN

Edward

'JUST MAKE SURE she gets it, won't you, Marie?'

'Of course, Master Fitzroy. But… Don't you think it would best coming from you? If you could just say goodbye and—'

'I don't think she's ready to be in the same house as me, let alone the same room.'

I eye the empty staircase as if I can somehow see her closed door, and beyond it her. Alone and avoiding me. Torturing me with her silence.

Two days since the ball and not a word. She's taken food to her room, had the entire household worried sick, and me… I can't stand it any more. Being so close to her and never more distant.

'No, it's better this way.'

Rufus whimpers at my feet. I'm not the only one she's shut out in her desire to cut ties, and as my hand falls to his head I feel the ache of it…

'I know. I know. I'll try and bring her back to you, I promise.'

'And what do I tell her if she asks where you are?'

'The truth,' I say to Marie, who's still unconvinced.

'Edinburgh's a big place.'

'And what does that matter? She's hardly going to hunt me down, no matter how much I might wish it.'

She simply stares back at me and I blow out a breath. 'I have a suite at The Balmoral.'

She nods, her eyes shifting to James as he approaches.

'Your car is ready, sir.'

His sombre expression is the same one worn by every staff member. Without Summer's sunny presence everyone is lost. But no one wants her back more than me…

'She'll come round, sir.' Marie's smile is full of encouragement. 'I just know she will.'

'I hope so, Marie,' I say, though I fail to muster a smile in return. 'I really do.'

One last glance up the stairs, hope that she will appear and put everything right giving me pause… But all I see is the ghost of a memory… her standing there two days ago, all ethereal and breathtaking. But that's all it is—a memory.

I blink it away, force one foot in front of the other as I seek to make things right the only way I know how.

Gran wanted Summer to make Glenrobin her home, and I'll do everything I can to make sure that happens…

Even if that means I'm the one who has to go.

Summer

I stare up the stone steps at the brass plaque on the wall bearing Mr McAllister's name and ignore my nagging conscience that's telling me it's the wrong man I've come to see.

Katherine's letter to Edward, handed to me by Marie at his request, is clutched in one hand, my letter from her is in the other, and I'm not even sure why I've bothered bringing them both.

They're identical.

Short, sweet and to the point. She's managed to write a personal message that's so specific and yet it fits us both.

I wonder if she suspected we would share them…that we would see them as a sign that we were meant to be. I can just imagine the sparkle in her eyes, the soft smile on her lips as she penned them to us.

The only change is her salutation. Both are signed off *Gran*. I only truly noticed when I had them side by side. Her way of including me in the fold even at the very end.

A solitary tear trickles down my cheek and I wipe it away.

What am I doing?

The question has been on repeat since I ran away from Edward, almost giving myself hypothermia in the process. If James hadn't found me when he did I dread to think what state I would have been in.

Not that I feel much better now.

The freezing wind whips my hair into my face, and I move before I make the same mistake again.

The warmth of the building envelops me, but the chill inside is impossible to shift. I find McAllister already waiting for me in Reception, and he takes me straight through to his office.

'Coffee, tea…something hot? You look frozen through?'

'I'm fine, Mr McAllister. Thank you.'

Though it's obvious I'm not.

'Call me Charles, please.'

I give a weak smile, a nod. 'Charles.'

He waves away his receptionist and ushers me into a seat. The same seat I occupied on my previous visit…only Edward isn't here now. I look to the empty chair, feel the emptiness inside me swell. I conjure up his face, his eyes, his smile…

'So, what can I do for you, Miss Evans?'

I drag my gaze to his, his friendly face a balm to my tormented soul. 'I need your help.'

His eyes drop to the letters clutched in my lap and I know he recognises them. 'That's what I'm here for.'

'I need you to tell me if there's any way I can sign away my rights to Glenrobin so that Edward can have it all.'

It's not what he's expecting, and his frown says it all.

'As I've already explained…' he interleaves his fingers, rests them upon his desk '…Katherine's wish was that you both live there for one year and then—'

'I know what Katherine wished...' my grip around the letters tightens '...but I can't live there.'

'I see.' He clears his throat, eyes me over his spectacles. 'Though I have to say, you and Mr Fitzroy seemed quite...*happy* with the situation at the ball last weekend. Do you mind me asking what's changed?'

Everything. Nothing.

'We were. Happy, I mean. But that was before...' I shake my head, empty it of Edward's declaration before it breaks me. 'It doesn't matter. I just can't live there any more, Charles, and I want Edward to be able to keep it.'

The silence extends between us and my heart throbs in my chest. What is the man thinking? Why isn't he speaking? Am I going to have to plead with him to help me?

'Katherine was a remarkable woman, Miss Evans. One of the most remarkable women I've ever met. And it seems she was also something of a soothsayer.'

I frown. 'A soothsayer? I don't understand.'

'This should explain it.'

He reaches into a desk drawer and pulls something out. He slides it across to me. It's like *déjà vu*. The same envelope as the two crushed inside my hand.

'Another letter?'

He nods. 'I'll leave you to read it in peace.'

'You don't—'

He's already rising, and as he passes he rests a gentle hand on my shoulder. 'Take as long as you need.'

And then he leaves, and the silence is so very heavy...the new letter heavier still...

Oh, Katherine, what are you doing to me?

I open the envelope, pull it out. My gaze goes to the grey outdoors as I take a deep breath and blow it out slowly.

And then I read, and I keep reading and reading and reading, the same paragraphs on repeat...

Dearest Summer,

I know you are scared. The day I met you, behind that brazen smile and tough attitude, I saw a scared little girl desperate to be loved and terrified of it all the same.

I should have stepped in all those years ago when I saw the magic you and Edward shared. It reminded me so much of what I had with Ben, God rest his soul.

We were together ten years before life cruelly took him away and, yes, it hurt. Ripped me apart. But would I have chosen differently? Would I have chosen not to love him and be loved in return? Never in a million years.

The truth is, going through life alone may well be safe, and it may well stop your heart from breaking, but your heart will never feel full or satisfied.

You will always be seeking the next adventure, Summer, until you realise that Edward is yours.

Open your heart to it. Let him in. And in turn he will give you the greatest adventure of all.

Make Glenrobin a true home again. Fill it with children, with dogs, with whatever your heart desires. But above all fill it with love and laughter and find your true happiness, my daring girl, because you deserve it all.
Love,
Gran x

I press a hand to my quivering lips but it's no good. I'm shaking from the inside out. Tears are streaming down my face.

This morning there was nothing, no scenario I could think of, that would have changed my mind, but I didn't anticipate this.

I feel like she's in the room with me, her eyes soft and sincere—hard and severe, too.

'Oh, God, Katherine.'

I stare at the paper, the words a blur. I've prided myself on my strength to go through life alone, to run when I need to, to protect myself because no one else will. To go on adventure after adventure, seeking a happiness that's always out of reach.

Not in Edward's arms, though. In Edward's arms I had it all—just as Katherine predicted. Happiness. Contentment. Love.

And I threw it all back at him out of fear when he chose to be so very brave.

'Oh, God, Edward...'

I shoot out of my seat. I need to get to him. I need to get to him now.

Please don't let it be too late.

Please, please, please...

Edward

'Is she in there, Charles?' I stride through his reception area, interrupt the conversation he's having with his secretary. 'Answer me, man.'

'Why, yes...' He straightens away from her desk, eyes wide with surprise. 'How did you...?'

'Glenrobin.'

It's all the explanation he needs. He knows I mean the staff. The staff who care about her, care about us, and know Gran's wishes through and through.

'I'd wait if I were you,' Charles says as my hand closes around the handle to his office door.

But I'm done with waiting.

I've left it a week, hoping, praying that she'll change her mind. That she'll come to me. Well, no more.

'Sorry, Charles, this needs to be—'

The door handle shifts in my grasp. The heavy oak swings open…

'Edward!' She's standing before me, frozen in place, pale, drawn, and never more beautiful to my Summer-starved gaze. The urge to sweep her up in my arms is painfully acute…sharper for the knowledge that I can't.

I kick the door shut behind me. 'We need to talk. I won't let you do this.'

'You're here…?'

'Yes, I'm here.' I pace before her startled form, unable to keep still.

'But why?'

'To do exactly what you're trying to do—gift the other half of Glenrobin and walk away.'

Her eyes flicker with some emotion that I can't identify. 'I *did* come here to do that. I *did* want to move on and leave you the house that I feel belongs to you… I *did*.'

'Did. Did. Did…' The way she keeps stressing it…it's driving me crazy. 'Are you *trying* to hammer the message home, Summer? Isn't it enough that I already know you don't want me? That you don't love me?'

'I never said that.'

'You did. Last week you said all that and more. Then tried to give yourself hypothermia in the process of leaving me. Do you know how hard it was not to come after you myself? To send James in my place?'

'I'm sorry for that, Edward…'

She says it so quietly and it hurts—it *really* hurts.

'Don't say sorry for that. It was my fault, I was the one without any patience, I was the one pushing you before you were ready—'

'Maybe I needed pushing…'

'—I shouldn't have said any of it. I shouldn't have—hang on.' I freeze. 'What did you just say?'

'I said…' She steps closer to me, her eyes wary, the nip of her lip warier still. 'I said maybe I needed pushing because for all I thought I was being brave, I was a coward.'

I frown at her, unable to speak.

'You're the brave one, Edward. Your childhood was no better than mine when it comes to parental love. You craved it and Katherine was the one who had to step in and give it to you. And yet you didn't let that fear of abandonment, of rejection, stop you from loving me. Not then and not now. You confessed your love for me, and out of fear I kept mine from you. I behaved no better than your mother, and for that I am deeply sorry.'

'Summer…?'

I can't catch my breath. I can't believe what I'm hearing…what she's implying. And I don't want—I don't want to feel like I felt a week ago. On a high, so in love, only to have it ripped away with such chilling force.

'Please, don't tease me, or beat around whatever bush this is. Because I don't think my heart can take a repeat of last week.'

'Good, because this isn't a repeat, Edward.'

She closes the remaining distance between us and lifts her hand. In it are letters—three if I'm not mistaken.

'Katherine sent me another letter. It appears she anticipated all of this.'

'Another letter?' I repeat, my voice hoarse, my head and heart struggling to keep up.

She nods. 'Do you want to read it?'

'Do you *want* me to read it?'

She gives me a smile so full of warmth and nods. Her cheeks are bathed in a sheen from the tears she must have shed before I entered.

I take it from her and it trembles in my grasp. 'Though if it caused those tears, I'm not sure…'

'*I* caused these tears, Edward. Our pain is my doing.'

My arms ache with the desire to hug her, to comfort her, to tell her she's wrong. But she's already backing away.

'Just read…and then I hope you will believe me when I say what it is I need to tell you.'

Hesitant, I lower my gaze to the familiar scrawl and read the words, feel the smile and the tears well.

'Dammit, she was shrewd.'

'Shrewd. Loving. All-knowing. She saw what I refused to believe all along.'

'And what's that?'

'That we're perfect for one another.'

I force myself to hold her eye. 'Is that so?'

Her nod is so slight, so hesitant.

I give a shaky laugh. 'You don't seem sure?'

'Because I'm worried it's too late. I'm worried I've hurt you too much…' Her brow puckers, her eyes swim. 'I'm sorry for throwing your love back at you. For not believing in you. And I'm sorry— I'm sorry for not being honest with you and brave enough to tell you that I love you too, Edward. Please forgive me?'

My heart tries to burst through my ribs. 'I'll forgive you on one condition?'

Her frown deepens. 'Which is…?'

'That you tell me again.'

'Which bit?'

I grip her hips, tug her to me with a growl. 'You know which bit.'

She laughs—the sound so joyous and happy.

'I love you, Edward! I love you! I love you!'

And I kiss her. I kiss her so deeply, and so passionately, and I claim what I've been missing all this time.

She breaks away far sooner than I'm ready, dropping back just enough to gaze up into my eyes. And softly now, with all the gravity the moment will allow, she says, 'I love you, Edward.'

'I love you too, Princess.'

Fresh tears well in her eyes. 'I don't think Katherine could have chosen my next adventure any better.'

'Nor mine.'

She tilts her head to the side, flashes a cheeky smile. 'Travel buddies?'

'I prefer the term husband and wife.'

'Deal.'

And she seals her promise, our elation, with a kiss.

Somewhere Gran is smiling down on us, a glass of sherry in her hand, toasting her greatest achievement. And I don't doubt the future she painted—not for one single, solitary second.

EPILOGUE

Three years later

Summer

THE SQUEALS OF excitement from the living room echo through the castle as Edward and I approach, our hands entwined.

'I think they've seen the presents,' I say, and he laughs.

'You reckon?'

Up ahead, Rufus comes tearing out of the room, a golden-haired toddler stumbling on his tail.

'Has he been?' I ask Lucy, whose eyes are like fishbowls, her curls bobbing around her head as she nods, her chubby hand pointing back towards the room.

'Santa!'

Her eight-year-old brother Liam skids up behind her, dragging along his six-year-old sister Lila. 'Summer! Edward! He's been! He's been!'

Lucy gives a piercing squeal and I wince up at Edward. 'Do you think that woke your parents?'

'With my father's snoring and my mother's earplugs, I wouldn't think so. This moment is all ours…until the sun comes up, at least.'

'Lucky us!'

My grin is so wide, my heart so full at the obvious joy in the children and the knowledge that this is to be our first proper Christmas with Edward's parents too.

The last few years have seen many a turnabout, especially where his mother is concerned. Her counselling sessions, and our family therapy sessions too, have helped to bring us closer together.

We're not the perfect family, not by far, but then I'm not sure such a thing exists…

We have our love, and that's what matters.

Especially today of all days.

'Well, we'd best go and take a look.'

Edward's palm is soft on my back as he encourages me forward. His brown eyes glisten in the fairy lights we've strung around the entrance hall, in amongst the holly and the ivy that I crafted with Carina, Marie, and our eldest foster child Lara.

'But where's—?'

And then I see her—Lara. She's hovering in the corner of the living room, her arms folded, her eyes wary as she takes in the tree with its array of presents beneath. She's the big sister, twelve going on twenty, and my heart aches for her.

Her smile is small when she sees us enter, her gaze on her siblings as they race for the tree, their excited chatter filling the air. It's our first Christmas as foster parents. Our first opportunity to give them the kind of Christmas I never thought possible when I was their age.

Edward squeezes my hand, and I give him a little smile before stepping away from him to go to her. We've come a long way since they joined us at Easter, and we've spent the build-up to Christmas feasting on all the traditions possible. Crafting, baking, carol singing, ice skating, a trip to see Santa… We didn't want to overwhelm them, but neither did we want Christmas to pass them by.

'Merry Christmas, Lara.'

I give her a tentative smile, pause a step away, and she lifts her gaze to mine. It's the tears I spy that steal my breath, and then her arms are wrapped around my waist, her head is on my chest.

'Merry Christmas, Summer.'

I hug her to me, kiss her hair, and try not to choke on the overwhelming rush of emotion inside.

I blink back the tears and spy Edward looking on, his smile full of love and happiness. He has Lucy in his arms, an excited Liam at his feet, and Lila is laughing as she rolls about with a barking Rufus on the floor.

It's noisy, it's perfect, and it's ours.

Thanks to Katherine.

Glenrobin—our family home.

* * * * *

If you enjoyed this story,
check out these other great reads from
Rachael Stewart

The Billionaire Behind the Headlines
Secrets Behind the Billionaire's Return
Surprise Reunion with His Cinderella
Beauty and the Reclusive Millionaire

All available now!